To:

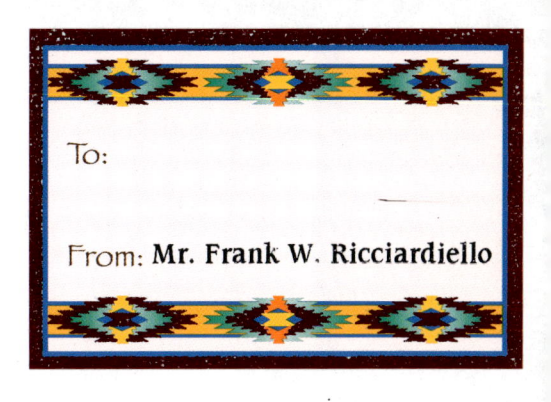

From: **Mr. Frank W. Ricciardiello**

Y0-DFL-943

NORTH SIDE STORY

Frank W. Pandozzi

Copyright © 2003 by Frank W. Pandozzi

All rights reserved. No part of this book shall be reproduced or transmitted in any form or by any means, electronic, mechanical, magnetic, photographic including photocopying, recording or by any information storage and retrieval system, without prior written permission of the publisher. No patent liability is assumed with respect to the use of the information contained herein. Although every precaution has been taken in the preparation of this book, the publisher and author assume no responsibility for errors or omissions. Neither is any liability assumed for damages resulting from the use of the information contained herein.

This is a work of fiction. Names, characters, places, and incidents either are the product of the author's imagination or are used fictitiously. Any resemblance to actual events or locales or persons, living or dead, is entirely coincidental.

ISBN 0-7414-1741-3

Published by:

INFINITY
PUBLISHING.COM

519 West Lancaster Avenue
Haverford, PA 19041-1413
Info@buybooksontheweb.com
www.buybooksontheweb.com
Toll-free (877) BUY BOOK
Local Phone (610) 520-2500
Fax (610) 519-0261

Printed in the United States of America

Printed on Recycled Paper

Published October 2003

This book is dedicated to a North Side friend.

Andrew P. Stein, Jr.

Andy was killed in Vietnam in the month of July, 1967.

I would also like to dedicate this book to all of the North Side fallen heroes of the Vietnam War.

May they rest in peace.

My deepest gratitude and thanks to some very important people.

The first person I would like to thank is Cathi A. Wong for her wonderful input on the color and design of the cover for this book. This is the second book cover that she has created for me and I am very thankful for her talent. Cat knows how to get inside my brain and remove the fuzz that seems to coagulate around my cover ideas.

The second person I want to thank is my copy editor Ava C. DeLorenzo. Ava met her challenge when she edited my book. I often tell people that I am a storyteller, not an English major. Ava worked a miracle and made my book readable.

The third person I want to thank is my wife Debra. Deb has had to put up with my moods, and my many sleepless nights while I was writing this book. She has also been my rock on which to lean upon.

Author's Comment

I feel that some explanation is in order. This book is a work of fiction. The names of the characters in this book are a product of my ever-consuming imagination. However, most of the events that take place are real events that actually happened. I had to change the names of the characters involved to protect the innocent as well as the guilty parties. I also feel compelled to mention that the names of the schools and places described are, in fact, the real names of each. I can cause no harm to places by using their real names. Also, I wanted to lend an era of authenticity to the book. If any reader who grew up in the city where this story takes place feels that a character being depicted in this book might be them, and should they feel embarrassed, then I am sorry. But remember, no one will know it is you, unless you tell them.

One

They called me Stretch. I grew up during the '50s and '60s on Back Alley, a dead-end street located on the north side of Syracuse. Syracuse is in New York State, the Big Apple. It is home to the Syracuse Orangemen and the Carrier Dome, and cultural diversity and fine restaurants.

Back Alley was a narrow street, approximately three city blocks in length. It became a dangerous street when two cars traveling in opposite directions had to pass each other. One vehicle would have to pull off to the side while the other passed by. Back Alley was one of the few streets in the city that had never been widened. I never could understand where Back Alley received its name. No one seems to know.

My house sat at the end of the street facing the street entrance. It stood proud, like a guard, protecting the entire street. I lived there with my parents, and my brother and two sisters.

Many of my friends lived on Back Alley. We were in trouble quite a bit. Because of our distinguished history among the Northsiders (as people who lived on the North Side were known), we were given the title of "The Dead End Kids" after the group of young gangsters that were portrayed in the movies of the 1930s.

That was a long time ago. Back Alley has since changed. The North Side has changed. I have changed. It was partly because of change that I had come back to the Alley and the North Side.

I sat in my car in the empty parking lot across from my old home, questioning my reasons for being there. It had been years since my family and I had moved from Back Alley. I had mixed feelings about what I was about to do. One feeling was anticipation; the other, a feeling of melancholy. The two conflicting emotions caused confusion. I was not sure what to expect from my trip back into my past. Nor was I sure that I would ever know why I'd come back. Here I was, a middle-aged man, with a wife and son, and a life completely different from where I had started, and I found myself being drawn back by a force that I could not explain.

As I stared at my old home, the memories came back to me. I remembered the house when it had been a proud structure. It had been built with care, using pristine oak and mahogany. Now it was rotting with decay and neglect. It was a reflection of the neighborhood's condition.

While sitting in my car, staring at the old house with broken shingles, I tried to remember those things that had been a part of my young life. I wanted to remember old scenes, but I was not sure why. Deep inside of me, there was a feeling that I could not explain. I sensed that there was a discovery to be made, and that discovery was waiting here, in my old neighborhood.

I'd tried before to go back to our house on Back Alley, to the neighborhood, to the North Side. It was where I had cut my teeth on life. In this neighborhood, I'd experienced the growing pains of youth. Many times, I had driven to Syracuse on business, and each time I had planned to visit my old home, but at the last moment, I'd always turned away. I was not ready, until now.

I slowly opened my car door. I had known for a long time that the old neighborhood was no longer a kind and gentle place. Crime and drugs filled the streets. I looked up and down the broken sidewalk; the alley was littered with trash. Slowly, I walked toward the old house; it called me to its doors.

The names of the kids who'd lived on Back Alley came back to me. My friends and enemies had names like Shooter, Boogers, and Scams. Their real names were Cosantine, Polanski, and Scambini. There were the Winkels, Hertzes, and Ragos, with nicknames like Manny the Crout, No-Nose, Louie the Lip, Snake and Knuckles. They called me Stretch because I was tall and skinny, like a pencil. I never liked the name, but the description fit me like a glove.

Back then, nicknames were important. They defined who you were. The names told others where you stood on the social ladder of the neighborhood. The uniqueness of your nickname determined how high you were on the status pole. It made no difference whether you were good or evil; if your nickname sounded like it demanded attention, then you were given respect and high ranking.

Some of the girls had nicknames also; this was usually because they were ugly, easy, or both. Pretty girls demanded too much respect, so they rarely were given nicknames. Sure, we called them foxes and hot mamas, but every adolescent boy who saw a pretty face, or a tight body, used those nicknames to describe the girls. A name like fox never identified any one girl; instead, it categorized all pretty girls.

Just as important as having a nickname was the fact that it was dishonorable not to call someone by his nickname. Having been blessed with a nickname by your North Side peers meant that it was understood you were to be called by that name. Whether or not you liked your nickname was not the issue; if given a name, you were stuck with it.

Most of the Northsiders wore their nicknames like badges of honor. They felt disrespected if addressed by their given names. Given names were for wimps. If you were a Dead End Kid, or a Northsider in our gang, you had to stand out among others. Birth names were okay for parents and teachers to use in our homes and in school and we understood that. But in the streets, we wanted to be addressed by our nicknames.

It seemed so strange that the neighborhood had changed in so many ways. Once Cosantines, Scambinis, and Palumbos had roamed these streets; now there were names like Wong, Nguyen, and Tran. Where small, mom and pop grocery stores owned by German or Italian immigrants had once stood, Vietnamese restaurants now replaced them. Phuong's Hair and Nail Parlor had replaced Carmine's Barbershop.

After a few moments, I began walking down the sidewalk of Back Alley. The sidewalk had once been used as a racetrack for my little wagon. I remembered persuading my younger brother and sisters to push me as fast as they could up and down Back Alley. I could hear their voices yelling at me to give them their turn with a ride in the wagon. Of course, I never did. I was the boss. I was the oldest and my word was the only word.

I walked down the long, red brick driveway between my neighbor's old home and my old house. As I walked down the driveway toward the backyard, I remembered the touch football games that had been played there. I remembered the baseball games in the driveway and the tennis balls that we'd used as baseballs. We would hit the balls down the long driveway toward the house in the backyard. My grandfather had built the tiny red house for a friend. He had owed him a favor, and the favor was returned by building him the home. That was a time when honor on the North Side was respected.

Standing there, I remembered how the ball would bounce off the tiny house, and the two old maids who lived there after my grandfather's friend had died would scream at us for "banging another ball off their home."

Stopping in the driveway for a moment, I stared at the broken and faded yellow shingles hanging loosely from the old house. I remembered breaking some of those shingles when a foul ball would scream off my bat. Of course, I would lie to my parents and blame the broken shingles on my little brother. I blamed him for many of my antics.

While staring at the broken shingles, I felt sadness for the old house. It was like an old person ravaged by time, and it was too late to repair the damage. The old home was dying a slow death.

I walked slowly down the driveway and toward the blacktop backyard. The first thing I noticed was how small the yard was. I had remembered it as being much larger, with room to run and play. But now, years later, the yard looked tiny. I wondered how I could have played back there. There seemed to be very little room to do anything.

I stared at the little red house where the two spinsters had lived. They had rented the house from my grandfather, and then after he passed away, they'd rented the tiny home from my parents. The old maids were always yelling at me for doing something wrong, even when I was doing something right. They would scream at me from their window, "Frankie, we're going to tell your mother." I didn't care. Nellie and Edith were old and harmless, so I ignored them and continued doing whatever it was that I was doing.

Looking around the yard, I recalled the small round swimming pool that used to sit in the middle of the yard. Although I could not swim, I did use the pool to terrorize my younger sister Kathleen. She could not swim either and was afraid of the water. So, I used to tease her by telling her that I was going to throw her into the pool and drown her. Teasing my sister was a passion of mine. I enjoyed watching her cry. One time I accidentally dropped a beautiful milk glass bowl that had belonged to my mother; it shattered into pieces. I blamed it on Kathleen and then sat back and watched my sister cry while my mother scolded her.

I noticed the old, cast-iron, red swing set that stood in front of the little red house. I was amazed that it was still there. My brother, sisters, and I had enjoyed many hours playing on that swing set. It consisted of two swings and a shootie-shoot that we used to slide down. The swing set had become rusted and broken, just like the old neighborhood and the house I used to call home.

As I looked around the old yard, I recalled the voices of the neighborhood. They were the familiar voices of The

Dead End Kids. I could hear Dickey "Axle Grease" Palumbo two houses away, "Come on over, Stretch and we'll do somethin'." Doing something with Axle usually meant getting into trouble.

We called him Axle Grease because of the large amount of white, creamy hair oil he put on his hair. Axle's hair was thick and black. He constantly combed his hair and carried a comb in the back pocket of his trousers. Axle had a curl that hung down to the middle of his forehead, "like Elvis," he used to say. He always wore a white tee shirt with the short sleeves rolled up to his shoulders. When he was older and could smoke, Axle would carry a pack of Marlboro cigarettes rolled up in his sleeves. "Just like James Dean," he'd told me.

I turned from the swing set and walked toward my old house just a few feet behind me. I looked at the three concrete steps that led up to the small porch that was the entrance into the back of the house. I remembered sitting on those steps many times with friends late into the night and talking about the New York Yankees, or the latest Topps baseball cards we had bought. The steps were now broken. Chips of concrete had peeled away, leaving large holes in the stairs that looked like caverns in the side of a mountain. I thought of the endless hours I had spent alone in the backyard throwing a tennis ball off the steps and then catching it before it hit the old maids' house behind me. I would pretend I was Mickey Mantle with the Yankees. I would imagine that each bounce of the ball off the steps back to me was a powerful hit by the great center fielder.

If the ball went high over my head behind me and then hit the old maids' house, it was a homerun. And again I would be screamed at for "bouncing the ball off the house." Hour after hour, I would bounce the tennis ball against those concrete stairs. It was my dream back then to some day be a New York Yankee. But, those dreams, like my old house and the old neighborhood, had become nothing more than memories.

Finally, I gathered the courage I needed to move forward. I wanted to walk up those stairs and onto the small porch that once led me into my home. I needed to experience feelings that had left me so long ago. I was unsure of what to expect once inside my old home.

Apprehensively, I knocked on the old oak door. The white paint on the door was peeling off, and the windowpane was cracked across its center and along the top. For a moment, I imagined I heard the voice of my mother calling me. I stood back from the door and laughed at the thought that my mind had just created an illusion. And then I heard the sounds my grandfather used to make as he worked in his woodshop located in the cold, damp cellar just beyond the door.

I stood there silently; I kept telling myself that it was okay. I was beginning to lose the courage I needed to knock on the door once more. A part of me wanted to turn and walk away. Suddenly paralyzed, I was unable to move forward and knock on the door, or turn and walk away. It seemed as if my feet were glued to the floor. I stood there, like a statue, on the front porch of my old home. While I was stuck in that spot, I wondered if anyone had noticed me standing there. I was hoping that no one had. I did not want a neighbor calling the police. It would be difficult for me to explain to the police what I was trying to do.

As I was about to knock on the door, it suddenly opened. A young Vietnamese girl, poorly dressed and dirty, her hair matted, stood in front of me; she was holding a baby. The courage came to me and I asked her if it were possible for me to look around my old house. At first, she was reluctant. I explained to her what it was I wanted to do. I told her I wanted to re-visit the house where I had grown up. Would she understand? I thought. The old house and neighborhood now belonged to her.

In the past, the oak door had opened to everyone. There was no need to worry about who was coming into our home. Strangers talked to strangers, and neighbors shared stories with others while their children played on the sidewalks. But, violence had replaced the neighborhood's old charm. The disease of crime had entered the old neighborhood and begun to destroy it. It was because of the crime that families needed to lock their doors and be wary of strangers.

Finally, after a few moments of indecision, the young girl allowed me into my old home. I thanked her and entered the hallway. In front of me stood the stairway that winded its way up to the second floor where my Aunt Rose and my cousins had once lived. The stairs and hallway still wore the same old, brown linoleum floor. The floor was cracked and sections were missing; it looked abused and neglected like the rest of the home.

I saw the stairs beyond the open cellar door that led down into the old cellar. Chills ran up and down my spine, just like when I was a child. Whenever Mom or Dad sent us down into the creepy cellar to bring up the laundry, or to get a jar of roasted peppers, or a bottle of wine from the wine cellar, it made our blood run cold. The cellar was creepy, but the wine cellar was even scarier. To us kids, it was the darkest and spookiest place on earth. Way back in the musty corner of the cellar was a room where my grandfather made his wine. I remembered the smell of old fermented wine that permeated the air. Because the wine cellar was located in the back of the basement, it was the longest walk from the stairs. I would often run as fast as I could to get to the wine cellar. I always feared that the bogeyman was hiding down there and he would grab me and do terrible things to my body. The wine cellar was the perfect place for him to hide.

As I looked down the hallway, the young girl told me to take as much time as I needed. I thanked her again, and she turned and walked into her kitchen. She had left the door open, and there I stood, staring into my past. I entered her kitchen and saw the same kitchen that had belonged to my mother. I could smell the aroma of my mother's spaghetti sauce cooking on the stove. It was my mother's stove. The same Magic Chef stove was still being used. Nothing in the kitchen had changed. It was dirtier than when my mother had owned it, but there was the same red and black linoleum floor, only faded. The old porcelain sink with its antique faucets still graced the wall to my right, and across and directly in front of me, on the back wall, was the old ironing board that folded out from the wall. I remembered spending hours standing there ironing my clothes, trying to impress all of the girls that I had loved with my neatness.

I turned to my right, walking past the old sink, and then stopped. The young girl had sat down at the kitchen table to feed her baby who was now crying. She was watching me; she'd noticed that I had stopped. I glanced at her and she must have read my mind. She nodded her head that it was okay for me to walk into the room that I had just approached. Walking slowly, I entered my old bedroom. It was here where I'd dreamed adventures and cried the tears of adolescence, and it was in this room that I had felt the safest. Walking slowly into the room meant going deeper into my past.

The girl came into the room with the baby in her arms and asked if everything was okay. Her presence surprised me and I sensed that she knew my feelings. I became embarrassed at the thought of her seeing my weakness. Suddenly, I just wanted to be alone. I wanted to remember the things that used to be and feel emotions that had been missing for so long. It had taken a lot of courage for me to come this far, now I needed to keep going. I asked her if I could sit on the bed, just for a moment. She told me that it was her young son's room and that he would not be home from school for a few hours. She then turned and walked out.

As I sat on the bed, I remembered the many hours I had spent here. This room had once been my sanctuary. It was where I had gone whenever the pains of adolescence had tormented me, where I'd cried when I was lonely, where I had dreamed of special places and of the heroes I'd wanted to be like. I remembered the hours of lying on my bed reading the statistics of every baseball card I owned. I recalled how I'd often played my electric football and baseball games here.

I thought about the nights when I would lay in bed crying because a certain girl did not like me, or because I was worried about my increasing acne problem. As I sat on the bed in my old bedroom, I stared at the walls of cracked plaster and faded paint. Again, I heard my mother's voice, calling to me to "get up for school."

After a few moments, I came out of the bedroom and went into the kitchen. The girl asked if I wanted to see the rest of her home. It was strange to hear her say that it was her home, but I was glad she had asked me. I nodded and followed her through the kitchen and into the dinning room.

As I walked from the kitchen, through the dining room into the front part of the house, I remembered that this had at one time been where my grandfather had lived until his death. Eventually after his death, and when I was still young, the rooms were remodeled. We moved into the entire first floor of the home.

While I stood in the front parlor, I remembered the time I had forced my younger brother Richard to get down on his knees and bark like a dog. I'd told him if he didn't, I would beat him until he did bark. Reluctantly, my brother had gone down on his hands and knees and began circling the room, barking like the good dog I wanted him to be. When I'd had enough of his barking, I petted his head and told him he was a "good boy." My brother had run out of the house crying.

And then there was the time I'd tried to force my sister Kathleen to eat a piece of my grandfather's moldy, aged provolone cheese. The cheese had little worms crawling through it. The worms looked like maggots. I told Kathleen that if she didn't eat the cheese, I would tell her friends that at age ten she was still wetting the bed. She never ate the cheese so the rumor about her bedwetting began to circulate around the neighborhood.

I walked to the front door that led to a front porch that extended the width of the house. The porch was enclosed with windows. I walked out onto the porch and looked onto the street that was once a familiar part of my life. I thought about the many evenings when I'd sat on the porch, watching the neighbors as they strolled by. I remembered the times I'd sat with my grandfather as he rocked in his rocking chair and smoked his long stinky cigar. Through puffs of smoke, he would scream at the kids in the neighborhood because they were making too much noise, or because they were running on his front lawn. Walking back to the front door, I looked up the winding stairway that had led to my aunt and uncle's home.

My Aunt Rose and Uncle George had lived upstairs on the second floor. My three cousins, Georgia, Carol and Peggy were their daughters. The old Italian tradition of families staying together was practiced by many families on the North Side. My Aunt Rose was my mother's sister, and along with their five brothers, they had grown up in the old house.

It was in this home where they and my grandparents had lived, maintaining as closely as possible the Italian culture that my grandparents had brought with them from Italy. My mother, my aunt and my uncles had grown up speaking both English and Italian. Italian was spoken between my parents when they did not want us to understand what was being said. I never understood enough Italian, except for a few curse words, to understand what information my parents and my aunts and uncles were at times hiding from us. Looking back, I am sorry I had not appreciated more the culture and the language of my ancestors. It would take me many years before I would finally understand this. I had known the people who'd lived in the neighborhood, but had never understood the true meaning of who they were and what they meant to the North Side. Going back home was a way for me to understand what I had missed, and remembering was sometimes painful.

The young girl met me in the hallway between the front door and the porch. Although she'd combed her hair and changed her clothes, she still looked dirty. I told her I had finished my visit and thanked her for allowing me to walk through my old home. I asked her if I could walk to the backyard one more time. She told me to go ahead and to take as much time as I needed. I walked across the front porch and down the stairs to the sidewalk. There was one more place I had to visit.

Behind the little red house was a small wooded area. Behind the woods was a fence that bordered the railroad tracks that came from the old candle company a few blocks away from Back Alley. This small wooded area had often been a retreat of mine. I had built a tree house there and used it to play in. It was a place of solitude where I would go when life was lonely. Like my bedroom, I would go there when I needed to solve my life's problems. The tree house had been torn down long ago, even the old elm tree where the tree house had stood had died. I sat down beneath a cherry tree that had been planted after we had moved away. Tears began to fill my eyes and roll down my face as I thought back to a time many years before.

Two

"Stretch, whatdya doin'?"

"Nothing, Axle."

"You wanna go to Skeleton Island?"

"Yeah sure. Let's go."

Axle lived two houses away from me on Back Alley. We used to call each other from our backyards. Only one house and a small fence separated us. As a shortcut to each other's house, we would climb over the wire fence. Our neighbor owned the fence. She was an elderly, widowed Italian woman, who was extremely religious and was always praying. Mrs. Santo felt the need to continually bless Axle and me. She would make the sign of the cross and say, "You boysa needa to goa to churcha more. Youa alwaysa ina trouble."

On that summer day, I was involved in my usual routine of throwing a tennis ball off the concrete stairs of my home. Axle was mixing some kind of rocket fuel formula he'd concocted from ingredients he had gathered from his father's garage.

I lifted myself over the fence and ran to Axle's house. I could smell the weird mix of chemicals he was stirring in an old cast iron bucket. When he smiled at me, I knew Axle was up to something.

"Stretch, this stuff is gonna blow the hell outta those carp."

"You're crazy, Ax. What if your old man comes home?"

"Naw. He ain't comin' home for a few hours. By that time we'll be outta here."

Axle poured the bucket of awful smelling rocket fuel into a half dozen canning jars and then hid them in the crawl space under the back porch of his house.

"There. My old man will never find it there. Maybe tomorrow we can go fishin' at Crap Lake for those big carp. You wanna?"

Axle had a weird sense of humor but he was my best friend. We did things together, good and bad, mostly bad. Usually Axle would influence me into doing things we should not have been doing. Most of his ideas for fun were spontaneous. That was Axle's problem. He never thought things through. Life to Axle was defined as instant gratification.

After Axle hid his rocket fuel under the back porch, we took two spuds for lunch from the refrigerator in Axle's house and headed toward our favorite summertime retreat, Skeleton Island. We never understood why everyone called the small wooded forest in the middle of Syracuse, Skeleton Island. Axle and I were there all the time and never saw skeletons, or bones of any kind. It wasn't even an island. The only water was a small swamp where Axle and I would go to shoot muskrats with our 22s.

As Axle and I walked to Skeleton Island on that hot summer morning, we decided to get a few ripe tomatoes to go along with our spuds for lunch. We used to love cooking the potatoes over an open fire. We would build a large fire, which we weren't supposed to do, and then drop the spuds into the flames. We liked our spuds burnt to a crisp.

"Hey, Stretch? Look at those babies over there," Axle said as he pointed to a row of large, summer-ripe tomatoes hanging from a vine. The tomatoes were in the backyard of a house we were walking past.

"You wanna get 'em? Or ya want me to pick 'em?" Axle asked as he stared at the beauties.

"I'll get 'em," I said. "You watch the street."

Quickly, I ran down the driveway and into the backyard. I picked two large, red tomatoes from their vines and ran back to Axle who was smiling from ear to ear.

"Wow, these beauties are heavy," he said as he took the tomatoes from my hands and held them up to the sky to get a better look.

Suddenly, the front door of the house opened. An elderly man began walking toward us, screaming and shaking his fists.

"You son–a-ma bitches. I'm gonna catcha you and kicka you assa."

Axle and I ran up the street laughing the whole time. We kept running until we were a few blocks away.

"That old man ain't gonna miss a few tomatoes," Axle said as he rubbed the red beauty he held in his hand.

"Boy, this is gonna taste real good with them spuds."

"Hey Ax? Let's take the shortcut?"

"Yea, good idea."

We crossed the street and cut across two backyards. As we ran across the final yard, we encountered a woman who was sitting on a swing with her young daughter. She was as surprised to see Axle and I as we were to see her. She started to scream at us to get out of her yard. Axle and I did just that. We ran all of the way to Skeleton Island.

We arrived at Skeleton Island around noon. The sun was bright and hot. Axle and I ducked into the cover of the small forest and immediately started a small fire. Within minutes we had a roaring blaze. We dropped our spuds into the fire and sat down on the ground staring at the flames. The smoke rose high and thick toward the treetops.

"I gotta take a leak," Axle said as he unzipped his pants.

"Hey Stretch, how far can you piss?"

Axle was shooting a long stream that flowed toward the burning fire.

"Come on, Ax. Don't piss on the fire."

He smiled at me and shook his penis. His piss stream splashed close to the fire.

"I bet I can put the fire out."

"If you piss on that fire, I'm throwing you in it," I told him.

"I'm just kiddin', Stretch. I wouldn't piss on our lunch." He tucked his penis back into his shorts and then took his comb from his back pocket. Axle combed his hair and adjusted the curl that hung down the middle of his forehead. When he was finished with his hair, Axle sat down next to me and reached into his shirt pocket.

"Stretch, look at these? I saved them for a special moment like this." He handed me a long fat cigar.

"Where did you get them?"

"I took a couple from the old man's pack. He'll never miss 'em."

Axle reached into his pocket and retrieved a pack of matches. The cigar hung from his mouth as he lit the end and deeply inhaled the smoke. He coughed and his eyes became red. His eyes began to tear as the smoke from the cigar swirled around his head.

"Whew, this is a good one," he said as he sat back against a tall oak tree.

"You gotta do it, Stretch." I stared at the cigar in my hand.

"You don't have any balls if you don't light it up."

Axle was puffing away on the cigar and talking at the same time. White smoke filled the air around us. Every few minutes Axle coughed and rubbed his red eyes.

Much to my dislike, I decided to light up. I knew if I didn't, Axle would harass me all day. I lit the cigar and inhaled the rancid smoke. My lungs began to burn and I coughed uncontrollably. Axle sat against the tree laughing. And then he blew a cloud of white smoke toward my face.

After a few moments of getting used to the fine art of cigar smoking, Axle and I leaned back against the old oak tree. We watched the massive fire as it crackled and roared while it cooked our spuds.

We sat under the cover of the trees talking about baseball, fishing and the neighborhood kids. Life was good when I was with Axle. At times, he'd angered me for some of the things he had done, but for the most part Axle had made me laugh. He was my best friend, but at that time, so long ago, I was not aware of him as being a best friend. He just happened to live two doors away from me. Axle just seemed to have materialized inexplicably into my life. I took him for granted, just like my bike and my fishing pole. I never questioned my friendship with him. I just assumed it was suppose to happen.

When our spuds were ready to eat, we jabbed them with sharp branches and pulled them out of the fire. They were burnt to a crisp, just the way we liked them. I reached into the pocket of my shorts and pulled out the saltshaker I had brought from home. We threw our cigars into the fire. Axle and I sat down against the large oak tree, sprinkled salt on both our spuds and the tomatoes, and feasted quietly. Suddenly, I felt a sharp pain on the back of my neck. I grabbed the spot on my neck that stung.

"I must have been bit by a bee," I said as I rubbed my neck.

As I sat there cursing the bee, Axle yelled in pain. He grabbed at his lower leg, below his shorts.

"Damn, I got stung too."

Then we heard laughing and the cracking of branches as someone ran through the woods behind us. As I turned to look, Axle yelled at me.

"Damn it, Stretch. Look at this?" He held out his hand and showed me a small, round BB in his palm.

"Some asshole's shootin' at us!" Axle screamed. He stood up and started running toward where we'd heard the laughing. As I ran after Axle, I could hear him cursing at the person who had shot us with the BB gun.

After a few minutes of running, I caught up to Axle who had stopped near the small swamp.

"The peckers are in there," he said as he pointed toward the field of cattails and goldenrod in front of us.

"I saw 'em run in there. There's two of 'em," Axle said, still rubbing his lower leg.

"I see ya. You asswipes."

Axle started running toward the cattails. I was rubbing my neck where the BB had smacked me.

My neck stung and I was just as mad as Axle was. I ran behind him. Axle could always run faster than I could. As I approached the field of cattails and goldenrod, I saw the two culprits running to my left. They each carried a BB gun.

Then Axle yelled again.

"You fagots. I see ya."

"Hey Stretch, it's those faggots, Manny the Crout and No-Nose."

"Okay Ax. Come on back. We know it's them; we'll get them later."

I could hear Axle talking to himself.

"Damn right I'll get the faggots. And when I do I'll rip their heads off."

Manny Winkle and his brother No-Nose were our enemies. No one in the neighborhood liked Manny or his brother. They were always in trouble at school, at home, or with the police. Whenever the Crout got into trouble, you could be sure that his brother Adolph Winkle was in trouble with him.

We called Adolph No-Nose because his nose was tiny and flat; it looked like the nose of a bull terrier. His nose barely protruded from his face. No-Nose and the Crout would do anything to cause trouble. And, they must have enjoyed being beaten up in fist fights, because that's what would happen to them whenever they were caught in one of their pranks.

"I'll get 'em, Stretch," Axle said as he rubbed his lower leg.

"I'll cut your nuts off!" he screamed in the direction of the two brothers.

"Come on. Let's get back to the shade," I told him. "It's hotter than hell in this sun."

We did not see the Crout or No-Nose anymore that day, but we knew we would see them eventually. Manny and No-Nose lived on Back Alley, across the street from Axle and me. It would be impossible to avoid them.

As Axle and I walked back to the shade of the trees on Skeleton Island, Axle was planning what he was going to do to the Winkle brothers. He had the rest of the summer to get even with them. I was sure he would.

Three

The winter months on the North Side were never wasted by Axle and me. We took advantage of the snow that would accumulate on the streets and sidewalks. We each had a Red Flyer sled and kept the runners waxed and ready. As long as there was snow on the ground, Axle and I would be on our sleds.

Our favorite place was the old North High School hill. The school was about a block from our homes. A long sidewalk twisted and curled its way up to the school from Back Alley. The sidewalk was a great place to race our sleds. If we had enough speed and hit the turns just right, we could glide all the way to our front doors. That was a test between Axle and me. The sled races between the two of us were fierce. Each one of us wanted to be the first to reach his house. We'd race each other hour after hour.

The sidewalk was only wide enough for two people to walk side by side. So, when Axle and I raced down the hill, we were right next to each other. Most of the time, we bumped into one another as we sped down the hill. If either one of us was bumped too hard, or we missed a turn, then we would end up going off the edge and down a very steep grade into a chain link fence. Sometimes, we ended up being thrown off our sleds as we skidded out of control down the embankment. But we would just wipe the snow from our clothes and trudge back up the hill, pulling our Red Flyers behind us.

Cars, buses, and trucks often sped down the street. Many times Axle and I had nearly been run over by a vehicle because we'd failed to maneuver the last turn. Just a few days after Christmas in 1960, the snow had fallen and covered the ground with fluffy, white flakes. Beneath this snow was five inches of packed snow. Axle and I knew the sledding would be good. We waxed the runners of our sleds and tugged them up the North High hill.

We started the race neck in neck. Going into the first and second turn our speed was increasing about the same; neither of us had an advantage. When we reached the third turn, Axle and I bumped sleds and he gained a slight advantage. He pulled ahead of me by two sled lengths and then went into the last turn very fast. Axle lost control of his sled as he tried to make the turn. He rolled off the Red Flyer and tumbled sideways, turning over about four times. I watched from my position behind him as he rolled into the street.

I held my breath as a city bus just missed running Axle over. I stopped my sled to see if he was all right; Axle got up laughing.

"Geez Stretch, that bus almost flattened me," he said as he shook the snow from his clothes.

After cleaning the snow from Axle's body, we trudged back up the hill, our sleds behind us, to continue our competition.

Axle and I participated in one even more dangerous winter activity. We would grab hold of the rear bumper of a city bus and have it pull us along the city streets. The best time to do this was when the streets had a thin layer of ice on them. We could slide along the streets for blocks at a time just by keeping a good grip on the rear bumper. Sometimes, we would hit a dry patch of street and would loose our grip and tumble over a few times. Fortunately, there'd never been a vehicle following too close behind us. We could have been killed or seriously injured. Most drivers would follow behind us at a distance.

Axle and I knew it was dangerous. Usually, it was Axle's idea and he would talk me into trying it with him. Skidding along the streets holding onto the back bumper of a bus always scared me, but Axle loved every minute of it. Most of the time, I would let go of the bumper first. Axle would just continue sliding along, not caring about the cars behind him, or the police, who might be in the area.

Axle told me that one time he'd caught the bumper of a city bus on the corner of Back Alley and slid behind it all of the way to downtown Syracuse, about twelve city blocks away. He said he'd held onto the bumper for over an hour without ever falling off or even seeing a police officer. He said the worse part was the exhaust fumes that had poured from the exhaust pipe.

During the winter, we used to go to the outdoor skating rink at McChesney Park. Young teenagers from the North Side would fill the skating rink. Some of them were good skaters; others were like me, uncoordinated. Just standing on the thin blades gave me trouble. But Axle skated well. He would glide along the ice like an Olympic skater. I would go to the rink just to watch the girls skate. I enjoyed watching them gracefully glide along the ice, especially the pretty girls with the cute figures.

Axle used to show off for the girls. He would streak along the ice and then weave between the pretty ones. Sometimes, he would show off by skating on one foot and then circle around any girl that was watching him. Most of the girls knew Axle, and that he was a showoff, so they either ignored him, or laughed at him. Everyone always had a good time, that is, until the Winkle brothers would show up.

They always seemed to be around. No matter what time of year it was, or what activity we were involved in, Manny the Crout and No-Nose were always there. They were never invited; they just enjoyed crashing people's good times.

The Winkles were average skaters; Manny was more coordinated than his brother. No-Nose had a problem with making turns on his ice skates. Actually, it was his inability to make turns that caused him and others on the rink problems. No-Nose would only skate in a straight line. When he had to turn, he would come to a complete stop, and then make his turn. Then he'd continue on his way skating in another straight line, until he had to make another turn. Then he would stop again.

One night, Manny and No-Nose decided to tease some girls who were ice-skating. Manny would frighten them by skating toward them, and then at the last minute, before pretending to slam into them, he would turn away. The girls would scatter and scream, calling him a freak, or an imbecile.

After watching his brother perform the daredevil act, No-Nose decided to try the routine. He started skating toward a group of girls who were standing in the middle of the ice rink. They were giggling and having fun when suddenly No-Nose came streaking toward them. One of the girls noticed him closing in on them and screamed to the others to move. As they moved away, No-Nose tried to stop but continued past the girls. Of course, he could not maneuver a turn, so he ended up slamming into Axle who was in a conversation with a cute girl who had just moved into the neighborhood. Axle and No-Nose both fell to the ground; both were sprawled out on the ice when Manny and I approached them.

"Whatdya doing, Winkle?" Axle asked as he brushed the ice and snow from his clothes.

"You was in the way," No-Nose answered.

Axle grabbed No-Nose and pushed him back onto the ice. No-Nose skidded along the ice on his back. Manny told Axle to leave his brother alone, and Axle pushed Manny to the ice.

"Now you guys were in my way," Axle said as he skated back to the pretty girl.

Manny and No-Nose were not going to let Axle off so easy. The two brothers left the skating rink and started home. Axle and I left a few minutes later. We were walking on the sidewalk and had just approached the old cemetery hill when Axle was hit with two very hard snowballs. After the initial shock from the attack, we turned our heads in the direction of the cemetery and saw Manny and No-Nose running back toward the rink.

"Damn you," Axle yelled while chasing after the two brothers.

Axle was screaming at the Winkles as he chased after them. "You guys are dead meat. When I catch you, you are DEAD MEAT."

That scene played out quite a bit on the North Side. Manny and No-Nose harassing Axle, and then Axle giving chase after them. It wasn't just Axle who chased the brothers; there was always someone pursuing them. No one liked them; Manny and No-Nose tormented everyone. They had no respect for anyone, or their possessions. They hated everybody and didn't have any friends. There was a joke amongst the neighborhood kids that even the parents of Manny and No-Nose disliked them. Axle and I always believed that story.

Four

"Aah ragsa. Aah ragsa." I remember hearing those words echo through the neighborhood when I was a child. They were sung by Antonio the ragman. He had a wagon pulled by his black and white pony Beppo. From the wagon, he would sell his rags to the women in the neighborhood. His wagon was always filled with rags.

Once a week, Antonio the ragman would travel through the North Side exchanging stories and rags with the people who lived there. The ragman knew everyone, and what was happening to each one. He loved children, and when we heard his words, "Aah ragsa, aah ragsa," we would run outside to greet Antonio and Beppo. Antonio carried candy to pass out to each of us. Sometimes, he would let us ride on his wagon or feed stale bread pieces to Beppo. I felt honored riding on top of the his wagon. I would smile and wave at my friends and neighbors. Antonio would let me yell, "Aah ragsa, aah ragsa." He told me that I would make a good ragman when I grew up.

Beppo always knew which way to go. He knew when to turn and when to stop. He knew the streets as well as Antonio. Antonio used to tell me that Beppo was the smartest pony in the world. He said Beppo was so smart he could add and subtract numbers, just like people. We would gather around Antonio's wagon and excitedly watch as he prepared Beppo for his trick. The ragman would tell us to be still and not to talk. Then he would show Beppo the cubes of sugar he held in his hand.

"Okaya Beppo. Youa ready?"

"How mucha isa two plusa two?" Then Antonio would show Beppo the cubes of sugar.

Of course wanting the sugar, Beppo would give a short neigh. But, Antonio, the genius that he was, would not give the sugar to him. So Beppo would neigh again. And again,

Antonio would tease Beppo with the sugar cube. And again he would ask, "How mucha isa two plusa two?" Beppo would again give a short neigh. Antonio would continue this routine until Beppo had neighed four times. And then, he would finally put the sugar into Beppo's mouth.

"Gooda boya," Antonio would say while rubbing the pony's head. We were always amazed at how smart Beppo was. It was not often that you had the chance to see a pony that could add or subtract numbers. And we made sure we told our parents about Beppo's mathematical abilities.

Sometimes Antonio would spend hours telling us stories about his life. He would tell us how he had come to this country on a large boat, just like my grandparents, and the grandparents of my North Side friends. Antonio said that his father had been a ragman in the old country, and he used to help him buy, sell and wash rags. Antonio had known no other way to earn a living when he came to the United States, so he decided to carry on his father's tradition.

He lived in the basement of a home on the North Side. He kept Beppo in an unused garage a friend owned. Antonio's life was simple. He never married. He said that he could not afford a wife or a family; it would not be fair to them to live with so few comforts. It was that kind of respect and loyalty to family that was the foundation of the North Side. Antonio the ragman was teaching the young children in the neighborhood, but at the time, we never understood it as such. The ragman's stories about his job, his simple living quarters and his life were told to us in an exciting way. No teacher has ever excited me as much as the ragman did.

I learned about the Great War, as Antonio called it, when our country had fought against the Germans and the Japanese. Antonio took me on a journey through World War II as he had witnessed it as a private in the Army. He told me stories of battles and honor, and of courage and death. The ragman told me why we'd fought the war, and why it had been important for him to join the Army. He told me that this country had given him so much, and he'd wanted to give something back. That attitude, about the love of his new country and the freedom it gave, also became the belief of all of the first- and second-generation immigrants on the North Side. Those hardy souls understood what freedom was, and how important it was to defend it. In this country, freedom was never taken for granted by the immigrants who settled here. They knew that if they worked hard and were honest, they would have an opportunity to provide for their families. Work and honesty were badges of respect worn proudly by the Northsiders. Words like honor, respect and loyalty were not only spoken, but were practiced.

When my grandfather did not have enough money to pay for my mother's wedding, he built a house of brick and mortar in his spare time as payment to the man he had borrowed the money from. When neighborhood women needed rags but had no money, Antonio would give them the rags knowing that payment would be made the following week. Neighbors helped neighbors and asked for nothing in return. There was a sense of pride in the community. That pride radiated like a beacon of light.

Although I did not know it at the time, Antonio was teaching me that having respect in one area of our lives extends in all directions. You cannot respect a neighbor's property while violating the rights of another.

Antonio had learned respect from his parents, as I had from mine, and as my friends had from theirs. They are lessons lost today. As I look around, I see little respect on the North Side. It only exists where the old-timers still reside. They are loyal and steadfast Northsiders. They resist the notion to move to the suburbs because of crime; they simply refuse to give in to the crime and disrespect that has taken hold of their neighborhood.

I was a teenager when Antonio died. He died in his sleep, a man without a family, but a man with many friends. Many people from the North Side attended Antonio the ragman's funeral. They came because of their respect, their loyalty, and their love for the man who could afford so little, yet who gave so much of himself to them. At times, I often wonder if Antonio would have the same effect on the residents of the North Side today.

Five

The Rago brothers controlled Franklin Elementary School. The brothers are a North Side legend. No family like the Ragos had ever entered the halls of Franklin School before them, nor has any since.

The three brothers were the definition of a thug. They began their lives as ruffians at a very young age, probably right after they were born. Franklin School had their first problems with the brothers when they were in kindergarten. By the time they were in the second grade, their reputations were already storied. My first experience with the brothers was when I was in third grade. That was when I was in Miss Humphrey's class. Miss Humphrey was a very large woman. She was also very old. And, when Miss Humphrey became the recipient of the three Rago brothers, it was her undoing.

The unique thing about the Ragos was not necessarily their mischievous natures, although, surely, their characters were unlike those of most other children of their age. What made it so much more difficult for the teachers was that the three brothers were triplets, and looked exactly alike. From their brown hair and their brown eyes, right down to their builds and postures, they were identical. And the Rago brothers used their identical looks to their advantage.

Louie the Lip Rago was the most talkative. He was loud and rude. Carmine Snake Rago was the hustler. By the age of nine, Snake already had a reputation for being a gambler. He was a card shark. He'd learned how to play "three card Monty" from his father. Snake used the game to cheat his schoolmates out of their milk money. Joey Knuckles Rago was the meanest of the three brothers. Although Louie and Snake never ran from a fight they'd started, Knuckles usually was involved in more of them. And to make matters worse, he would beat his young opponent unmercifully, usually until the hurting youngster begged forgiveness.

Knuckles would start fights for all kinds of reasons. He was also known for kicking his teachers in the ankles and spitting at Mr. Pinkley, the school principal—like that time in Miss Humphrey's third grade class. All four of us had Miss Humphrey's for a teacher that year.

It was the first day of a new school year. Our third grade class was involved in a reading lesson when someone, probably one of the Rago brothers, passed some gas. It sounded like an explosion. Of course, all of us began to laugh. Miss Humphrey, who'd also heard the explosion, scolded the class for laughing at the repulsive act. As Miss Humphrey was trying to calm the class down, there was another loud purging of gas, even more pronounced than the first.

Once again everyone in class laughed. Again, Miss Humphrey yelled at us for laughing at such a vulgar act. Then, Louie the Lip screamed out for all to hear, "Hey teach, did you fart?" The class broke into laughter and Miss Humphrey again scolded us. She told Louie to keep his mouth shut and to read the next paragraph. Instead, he said, "I ain't readin' it. You read it."

Snake and Knuckles were seated behind me, but in front of Louie the Lip. They jumped up and down in their seats and stomped the floor. Miss Humphrey said she'd had enough and told Louie to go to Mr. Pinkley's office. He told her that he was not going, then let go another bomb. This one was even more powerful than the first two.

Knuckles and Snake were beside themselves. The class was in an uproar, and Miss Humphrey was very angry. The big woman walked over to where Louie was seated and pulled him from his desk. He kicked her in the shins. Knuckles and Snake yelled to their brother to kick her again. Miss Humphrey wrapped her fleshy arms around Louie and, in a bear hug, carried him out the door.

The class was still laughing at what was happening when Knuckles stood up and told everyone to shut their mouths, or he was going to shut them. Immediately, the class became quiet.

After Miss Humphrey had Louie situated in front of Mr. Pinkley, in his office, she came back to class and resumed teaching. While in the principal's office, Louie the Lip spit at Mr. Pinkley. He told Louie that he wanted him to apologize to Miss Humphrey and the class. Louie would do no such thing, so he was thrown out of school.

It was not the first time one of the brothers had been banished from school. At least once a year, one or all of the brothers were expelled. In any case, none of the Rago brothers got further than the seventh grade. They decided they had learned enough and were old enough to leave school. Most of the North Side kids had moved past the three brothers years earlier. By the time Louie, Snake and Knuckles had reached the sixth grade they were shaving. And, by the time they were in seventh grade, the joke was that they were almost old enough to vote.

By the age of eight, Snake was a magician with cards. He could trick anyone, even most adults, with his quick, slight of hand card tricks. "Three card Monty" was his favorite trick. He would show the black ace to an innocent kid and ask him or her to watch it closely and then find it amongst the other two cards. Then Snake would shuffle the three cards and throw them face down on the floor. Of course, the first time he would show the trick in a clumsy slow manner, baiting his prey. Most often, the kid would find the black ace the first time, proudly pointing the card out to Snake.

Snake would turn the card over and say something like, "Geez kid, ya found it. You're good. How 'bout we do it again? This time kid, bet ya a dime ya can't find the black ace."

Of course, the youngster had found the black ace the first time and was confident he could do it again. It was also a chance to win a dime. Swiftly and smoothly, Snake would pass the three aces over and under his hands and toss them on the floor face down.

"Where's the ace now, kid?" Snake would ask confidently.

The poor kid, who had just tossed his milk money down on the floor with confidence, suddenly became confused, with no idea where the black ace had gone. The bettor would stare at the backs of the cards thinking that they'd seen the black ace fall in the middle of the three cards lying there, or perhaps it was the card on the right. Then again, they would think, maybe it's the card on the left. And, of course, they would choose the wrong card and Snake would win another dime.

During Mr. O'Reilly's fifth grade class, Snake was caught playing "three card Monty" in the boys' restroom. He would always carry the three aces tucked away in his shirt pocket, ready to take advantage of some poor unsuspecting kid with lunch money.

The incident in the boy's restroom was nothing new for Snake. The restroom was where he did most of his gambling. One time, Snake had some poor kid in tears. He'd taken the little guy's lunch money and his Mickey Mantle baseball cards. Knuckles and Louie the Lip were in the restroom cheering their brother on. Everyone was sitting on the floor in front of the urinals. The crying gambler had three of his classmates with him; they were rooting for him. It was a carnival-like atmosphere in the restroom.

Suddenly, two teachers walked in and broke up the game. Snake had to give back the money and the Mickey Mantle cards. Then Snake was told to go to Mr. Pinkley's office. The brothers thought that it would be a good time to have some fun. Instead of Snake going to see Mr. Pinkley, Knuckles took his place.

Mr. Pinkley was tired of the brothers and their pranks.

"Young man, what have I told you about playing cards and gambling?"

The two teachers who had walked into the restroom were standing next to Knuckles, who was standing in front of Mr. Pinkley's desk.

"I weren't playin' cards."

"You mean, I was not playing cards."

"That's right. I weren't playin' cards."

"You were caught playing cards and gambling in the restroom. Is that not correct?"

"It weren't me."

"Are you saying that Mr. Olsen and Mr. Crenshaw are liars?"

"Yup."

Angered, the two teachers looked at Knuckles, who they thought was Snake.

"If you were not gambling, then what were you doing?"

"Takin' a piss."

"You mean you were urinating?"

"Yup. Urnatin'."

Mr. Pinkley would have no more of the nonsense displayed by the child he thought was Snake Rago. Shaking their heads, Mr. Olsen and Mr. Crenshaw returned to their classes, and Knuckles was dismissed from school. He was glad for the day off. However, Knuckles was more glad because he had fooled Mr. Pinkley into believing that he was his brother.

Every day the Rago brothers harassed their schoolmates. Ernie Frump was a small, delicate kid who was afraid of his own shadow. Ernie wore a hat to school everyday. It was the type the Frenchmen wear, a beret. The beret was red, and he wore it during the spring, fall, and winter months of school. The red beret was a part of Ernie's personality; we accepted Ernie Frump and his hat.

Ernie was not allowed to wear his hat during school hours. When his beret was not on his head, he would tuck it into his back trouser pocket. It was common to see Ernie walking through school with his hat swinging from his rear pocket. One day, the three Rago brothers decided to have some fun with Ernie Frump and his hat.

It was lunchtime and Ernie was walking to the cafeteria when Louie the Lip, Snake, and Knuckles spotted him. The three brothers were bored, so they made Ernie their target. As they walked behind Ernie, Knuckles grabbed Ernie's beret from his back pocket and began running down the hall, waving the hat in the air. Snake and Louie followed their brother outdoors. Ernie was not sure what to do. He knew that if he went after his hat, the brothers would probably beat him up, but he loved his hat and he wanted it back. Ernie decided to follow the brothers outside and see if they would return his beret.

Knuckles was outside wearing the red hat and showing off to his brothers by dancing around the schoolyard and acting silly. They were laughing and making jokes about the hat. Louie the Lip called it a sissy hat. They were having a good time with the hat when Ernie nervously approached them. The brothers were passing the hat back and forth between them. Each one took a turn at placing the red beret on his head. Ernie timidly walked up to Snake who was wearing his hat.

"Hey, look who's here," Snake said. He was dancing around the school parking lot showing off like his brother had done. Ernie wasn't sure which brother was talking to him.

The children on lunch break were standing outdoors and watching what was happening between Ernie and the Rago brothers. Most of them moved closer to get a better look. There were no teachers around at the time.

Ernie stood silently. He was scared and wasn't sure what to say to the Rago brother who was wearing his hat. He was hoping that the brother would give him his hat back without beating him up.

"I like dis hat, Frumpie," Snake said. "I'm gonna keep it."

"Naw, I want it," Louie told his brother and grabbed the hat from his head.

Louie the Lip began running toward the far end of the parking lot. Everyone followed him. Snake managed to catch up to Louie and snatched Ernie's hat from his brother's head. He tossed the beret to Knuckles, who then threw the hat back to Snake. The brothers were playing "keep away" with the beret.

Ernie watched silently as Snake ran between his two brothers trying to catch the beret. He wanted to say something but didn't have the courage. Some of his schoolmates told Ernie to go after the hat, but Ernie was too scared.

"Hey Frumpie," Louie the Lip yelled out, "wheredya git the sissy hat?"

Ernie finally decided to confront the brothers. He still was not sure which brother was holding his hat. He was afraid to say their names. If he mistakenly called them by the wrong name, he knew he would be in big trouble.

"Can I please have my hat?" he asked in his squeaky, polite voice.

"Whatdya say, Frumpie?" asked Knuckles, who was wearing Ernie's hat.

"Can I please have my hat?"

"Hey guys, it talks," Louie told his brothers.

"You want your hat?" Knuckles asked as he removed the beret from his head. "You gotta come and git it, Frumpie."

Ernie was looking for help from his schoolmates. But no one wanted to mess with the brothers. So, Ernie stood there, waiting for some courage.

"Hey guys," Louie said, "let's see if he knows who we are?"

"Yea. If Frumpie's right, we'll give 'em his funny lookin' hat back," Knuckles said. Snake agreed.

The brothers lined up shoulder to shoulder in front of Ernie. The crowd of children watched quietly as Ernie stared at the three brothers. Some of the kids whispered among themselves and tried to guess where each of the Rago brothers stood. Then Louie told the children to keep their mouths shut or he would turn Knuckles loose on them.

"Ya gotta get all three of us right, Frumpie," Louie yelled out.

"If he's wrong," Knuckles added, "we git ta tear up his beanie."

"Yea. We'll tear up Frumpie too," Snake taunted.

The Rago brothers laughed and told Ernie to get on with it. Ernie was scared; he was afraid to call out their names. He knew he would be guessing. He wondered if getting his hat back was worth it. The three brothers urged him on; they told him if he did not make a decision soon, they would tear him and his hat anyway.

Ernie began to cry. He was too scared to talk, and he was too scared to run away from the brothers. Because Ernie began to cry, it saved him and his hat. To see delicate Ernie Frump cry was good enough for the Rago brothers. The bullies had accomplished what they had wanted. Knuckles gave Ernie his hat and pushed him to the ground. Everyone went back into the school as lunch was over.

Ernie was all alone. He was still sitting on the ground where Knuckles had pushed him. He wiped the tears from his eyes and tucked his red beret into the back pocket of his trousers. After a few minutes, he stood up and walked back into Franklin School. Ernie Frump had accomplished what he'd wanted as well; he had gotten his hat back.

Many years later, after our graduation from high school, most of the Northsiders had heard that all three of the Rago brothers had been locked away in prison for various crimes. I don't believe that any one of us was shocked by that news. We'd known that it was just a matter of time before the Ragos would finally meet their match.

As for Miss Humphrey, she retired from teaching at the end of that school year. The Rago brothers had been too much for her. She was never up to teaching again. She moved away to Arizona, and shortly thereafter, died of a heart attack.

Six

"Stretch, a bunch of guys are gonna play ball at the North High School field, get your glove."

Scurvy Sam Giambollo was a friend of Axle's and mine. Everyone called him Scurvy because his face had large red pimples. Scurvy was a very good baseball player. He hit the ball easily, without effort. He loved the game and was always starting one, gathering the kids from Back Alley and around the North Side then picking where we would play. When Scurvy approached me, I was in my backyard painting the outdoor window casings on the old maids' house. My mother had given me the job before she'd left for work that morning. She told me that I had better get the job done before I went anywhere with my friends, or else. Instead, I quickly put the paintbrush in a can of turpentine, grabbed my baseball glove, and went with Scurvy to pick up Axle at his house.

When we arrived at the high school ball field everyone was there. They were warming up by tossing baseballs back and forth. Joey Cosantine, who we called Shooter, was also there. We called him Shooter because of his talent of beating anyone at flipping coins. We pitched coins all the time, and usually Shooter came out the winner.

Freeman Buggers Polanski was also warming up. The Northsiders called him Buggers because his nose always dripped snot, even in the summer. The snot would become dry and crusty and cake up on his nose and upper lip. Buggers was constantly wiping his hands across his nose to clean the mess. Sometimes, he would pull up his tee shirt and blow the snot into the underside of it, and then roll the shirt back down. Freeman was not the brightest kid, and he had a bad case of stuttering. Most of the time, we never let Buggers finish what he was saying because it took him too long.

Little Nicky Scambini, who we called Scams, was at the ball field playing catch. We called him Scams because the nickname seemed to fit. Little Nicky was a tough street fighter. He was only five feet tall, but he was one of the strongest kids on Back Alley. He loved to start fights and would usually come out the winner.

Two Toes Sam Molletti was playing catch with Scams. Two Toes was Scam's best friend and just as tough as Scams. We called him Two Toes because we'd heard that he had been born with only one toe on each foot. Of course, Two Toes never let anyone look at his feet, so we weren't sure.

Jimmy Skidmarks Bartolo was at the ball field arguing with Boogers about who was going to play first base. Jimmy was called Skidmarks because he was always crapping in his pants. We could never figure out why Skidmarks did that. He would always have an extra pair of underwear stuffed into the pocket of his blue jeans for emergency purposes.

Baby Face Cosmo Cosantine, Shooter's younger brother, was just walking up to the baseball field when we arrived. As a joke, we called Cosmo Baby Face because he was so ugly.

Harry Armpits Hertz was standing by himself on the pitcher's mound waiting for someone to throw him a ball. Harry was nicknamed Armpits because his arms were long and wiry. We used to say that his arms looked like monkey arms because they hung almost to the ground. Armpits figured he was the best pitcher in the neighborhood. Scams agreed and told him that he was going to pitch this game for one team and Two Toes was going to pitch for the other team. No one wanted to argue with Scams, so there was no debate over pitching.

Sometimes we would play homerun derby. Each one of us took turns at having someone slow pitch to us. We would hit the ball as hard as we could. The object was to hit it over the North High School fence. The person who hit the most homeruns won the contest. Usually Scams won. Not only would he hit the balls over the fence, but he would drive them onto the walls of the school. The school was approximately fifty feet beyond the fence. Sometimes, the ball would crash into the school windows breaking them. Scams was a man among boys when it came to batting; he made it look easy. He could bat from both sides of the plate, just like Mickey Mantle.

Shooter and Axle were good baseball players also. Shooter was as quick as a rabbit. With his speed he could hit a single and turn it into a double. He could hit any pitch thrown to him, and no one could strike him out. Axle was the same kind of hitter. He was not as fast as Shooter, but he got on base often. Axle was also a good outfielder. He always knew where the ball was. Whether it was a ground ball or a long fly, Axle would get to the spot and make the catch.

That day, we decided, as usual, that the two captains would choose sides. We named Axle and Scams the captains for each team. Axle was chosen because he was a good ballplayer and Scams was chosen because if he was not chosen a captain, he would want to fight whoever had been chosen.

When choosing players for each team, there was usually disagreement. Not everyone was happy with their team. No one wanted to be on the same side as Boogers. Boogers was a terrible baseball player. He never hit the ball, so he was always a strike out for his team. His fielding was terrible. Most of the time, Boogers played right field because that was where the least amount of balls were hit. When the ball was hit in his direction, he would run after it yelling, "I ga-ga-got it." He would usually misjudge the ball and miss the catch. Sometimes the fly balls would come down on his head. One time, Boogers broke his snot-filled nose when a pop fly he was running under bounced off his face.

But as bad as he was, Boogers could always be counted on to play. He loved baseball. Many times he would be seen walking from park to park looking for a baseball game to play in. And he always carried his trademark Ted Williams baseball glove with him. Even when not playing in a game, Boogers would walk around wearing his glove, like a proud professional. He never took it off. When snot dripped from his nose, Boogers would wipe it with his glove hand. He was an avid Boston Red Sox fan. Along with his trademark Ted Williams glove, he wore a Red Sox baseball hat. The hat was dirty and stained, and it never sat squarely on Boogers's head. The brim always pointed toward one of his ears.

We choose sides and played one inning, and then Manny and No-Nose showed up with their baseball gloves. They were standing behind the backstop. Axle was the catcher. When he heard the two brothers laughing at Boogers, who was standing in right field picking his nose, Axle threw down his glove and began to chase them. He screamed at them as he chased them all over the ball field.

"You're dead meat. You peckerheads."

We yelled at Axle to get back to the game. But he was still mad from the BB-gun incident. Finally, Axle caught No-Nose, who was the slower of the two brothers. No-Nose had tried to climb the six-foot wire fence that surrounded the ball field. Just as he was on top of the fence and ready to jump to the other side, Axle grabbed him. No-Nose fell to the ground and began crying. He always cried when he was about to get beat up. It was a means of defense, and he used it often. Sometimes it worked, but most times, he would still get beat up. However, Axle knew No-Nose too well, and he knew his tricks. Axle dragged him all the way back to the baseball diamond and set him on the pitcher's mound. He asked if any of us wanted to take a swing at No-Nose before he "beat the crap outta him."

In the meantime, Manny the Crout had run off and hid, leaving his brother at the mercy of Axle and the others. Axle let No-Nose cry for a few minutes and then slapped him on the head, as a warning for the next time.

After Axle let No-Nose go, the rest of us began to walk off in separate directions. Shooter walked over to me, he was pinching his nose.

"Damn, Skidmarks crapped his pants."

Skidmarks came walking toward us.

"Get outta here," Shooter yelled.

Skidmarks was squeezing his ass with both hands. "Aw, come on guys. Let me walk with you. I changed my underwear and threw 'em in the bushes."

"Get outta here, you stink!" Shooter screamed back, still pinching his nose. Skidmarks turned and walked away in the opposite direction.

As usual, the game had never ended—that happened often. Someone would start an argument over a ball that was a strike, or someone would pick a fight with someone else over a little incident, and the next thing you'd know the game was being cancelled. Usually, it was Scams or Two Toes who started the fights.

Two Toes Sam Molletti was the tallest Northsider. He was also one of the meanest. I was six feet four inches tall, but Two Toes towered above me by at least five or six inches. He played basketball in school and at the CYO (Catholic Youth Organization) recreational league, where most of us played.

One Saturday morning we were playing a CYO basketball game against some kids from the southwest side of the city. Our team consisted of Axle, Two Toes, Shooter, Harry Armpits and myself. Boogers was a sub. He was sitting on the bench watching us and trying to pick his nose while wearing his Ted Williams baseball glove.

We had the ball out of bounds and underneath our basket. I in-bounded the ball to Shooter, who dribbled down the court. He passed the ball to Two Toes, who had snuck in behind the defender underneath the basket. As Two Toes caught the ball and went up for a shot at the basket, he was hit in the face with an elbow of one of the defenders. Two Toes wasted no time in grabbing the kid by his tee shirt and throwing him onto the court. While he beat the defenseless player, the player's teammates rushed to his aid.

Father John, a short, stumpy priest, and two nuns, Sister Mary Margaret and Sister Carrie Angeline, were supervising the game. The three clergy, and the rest of our team, ran onto the court and tried to break up the melee.

When the fight was broken up, Two Toes had a swollen eye, but the player who'd accidentally slammed his elbow into Two Toes's face was badly beaten and had to be taken to the hospital. Sister Mary Margaret yelled at Two Toes and slapped him with her notebook. She told him that she was not allowing him back into the CYO until he memorized a section of the Bible. Sister Mary Margaret's word was the law. If you did not obey her word, then you would pay the consequences. Everyone feared her, even Father John.

Sister Mary Margaret was more of a drill instructor than she was a nun. She was mean and authoritative. The North Side kids who were unfortunate enough to go to the Catholic school where she taught were not envied by any of us. For myself, and most of the gang I hung out with, the only time we were in the presence of Sister Mary Margaret was when we were playing ball at the CYO, or on Tuesdays at church school.

Church school was for any Catholic student who did not attend a Catholic school. Once a week, we had to leave our school early and walk to one of the Catholic schools on the North Side. It was at church school where many unfortunate students would end up with Sister Mary Margaret as their church schoolteacher. If you were given a Bible lesson and it wasn't finished, Sister would yell and scream and cause a terrible disturbance. And, if we were unruly, Sister Mary Margaret would crush our knuckles with her heavy ruler.

Axle and I had Sister Mary Margaret for a teacher three years in a row. Even though we only saw her once a week, it was still too much. And we never completed our bible lessons. So Sister Mary Margaret spent much of the time beating our knuckles with her ruler. One time she smacked Axle so hard she broke the ruler. When she caught me laughing, she slapped my face and sent me to see Father John.

Father John was a pushover. He was the priest in charge of the church and the school. He was easygoing and never yelled at anyone. All of the students liked Father John. When Sister Mary Margaret sent me to see him, I went home instead. I knew that Father John would not know that I was supposed to see him. Sister Mary Margaret always forgot to check with him anytime she sent a student to see him. Besides, I knew that Father John would just tell me to try and be more respectful next time.

Seven

Before I became a teenager, I became a Boy Scout. I'd joined the Scouts because I thought it would be fun; instead it turned out to be a disaster.

Axle and Shooter and I joined the Scouts together. Manny the Crout and No-Nose were already Scouts, and all of us ended up being in the same troop and patrol. Our Scout leader was Mr. Dunwell. We used to make fun of his name. Sometimes we would call him "Mr. Well-Cooked," or "Mr. Crispy." Mr. Dunwell did not appear to be the outdoors type. He was a sissy-type looking man. He always reminded me of Mr. Peepers, the skinny, beanie-eyed character on TV in the 50s. Mr. Dunwell looked just like Mr. Peepers. He had the same skinny frame and wore thick, black-framed glasses. In addition, his head was much too large for his skinny neck. Mr. Dunwell's head never looked like it was secured to his neck. I used to think that at any minute it would fall.

Mr. Dunwell was very proud of the Boy Scouts, and he showed it by wearing his Boy Scout uniform wherever he went. He used to spit shine his Boy Scout shoes and polish all of the badges he'd received over the years. He'd become an Eagle Scout at a young age.

Mr. Dunwell was a pushover. We abused the poor man. Axle loved to tease him. Everything that Mr. Dunwell would ask Axle to do, Axle would do just the opposite. If he asked Axle to tie a square knot, Axle would tie a hitch knot. If he asked Axle to follow the compass in a certain direction, then Axle would intentionally go in the opposite direction. One time, Mr. Dunwell had to call out a search party in the woods to look for Axle. We were on a Boy Scout weekend in the Adirondack Mountains in New York. Mr. Dunwell had told Axle to follow his compass east out of the woods to a predetermined meeting place. Axle intentionally went west a short distance. When Axle did not reach the meeting place at the specified time, Mr. Dunwell organized the search team. Axle hid in the woods, watching Mr. Dunwell scratch his head as he called Axle's name.

Axle was our patrol leader. Our patrol consisted of Axle, Shooter, Manny, No-Nose and myself. Mr. Dunwell told us many times that we were the worst patrol he had ever seen. He'd tried very hard to make us the best patrol, but it never happened. One of the problems was that none of us had a very long attention span. Today, the experts call that problem "attention deficit disorder." When my friends and I had the problem in the 50s and 60s, there was no name for the dysfunction. Back then, the Back Alley Boys and I could have been the poster children for the disorder. Mr. Dunwell had known for quite some time that we had something wrong with us. He tried very hard to help us conquer our lack of attention problem. But, he was just not the right type of person to help us to become more useful individuals.

We argued often at our patrol meetings. That was because Manny and No-Nose were part of our group. Mr. Dunwell had given our patrol the two Winkle brothers because we were the smallest group. He made a very bad mistake by bringing Manny the Crout and No-Nose into our close-knit patrol. We decided we would make him pay the price for sticking us patrol with the Winkle brothers.

It was in February, and we were at a Boy Scout camp for a weekend. Our entire troop of fifty Boy Scouts and a dozen fathers were staying in log cabins that slept twenty Boy Scouts each. There were four cabins available. It was a cold February in the Adirondack Mountains, so we had to keep hot food cooking and the wood stove filled with burning hardwood logs. At night, the temperature dropped below freezing. It was Axle who came up with the idea to pay Mr. Dunwell back for bringing Manny and No-Nose into our patrol. Shooter and I agreed to Axle's plan, which we were to carry out that evening after everyone had gone to sleep.

Mr. Dunwell was a sound sleeper, which made it easy for us to carry out our plan. Shooter, Axle, and I waited until everyone in our cabin was sound asleep. Mr. Dunwell was snoring loudly as he lay in his cot next to the wood stove. He was the only adult in our cabin that evening. It was one o' clock in the morning. The wind was howling through the trees, and a light snow was beginning to fall. Shooter and Axle retrieved the rope they had hidden beneath their bunks; we were ready to begin.

Slowly, the three of us approached the sleeping Scout leader. Axle and Shooter quietly wrapped the rope around his body and his cot. After securing the rope with a Boy Scout knot that Mr. Dunwell had taught us, we slowly picked up the cot and carried him outdoors. After carefully putting Mr. Dunwell on the front porch of the bunkhouse, we went back indoors, locked the front door with the cast iron latch, and went to bed.

We fell asleep and never woke up until a few hours later when we heard our Scout leader yelling as he pounded his fists on the front door. We unlocked the latch and let him inside. Mr. Dunwell was cold but not frostbitten. He was mad but never questioned any of us more than once about who'd tied him outdoors. He never punished anyone for the prank. In fact, no one ever found out who'd tied Mr. Dunwell to his cot. It had remained a secret, until now.

Axle, Shooter, and I were eventually thrown out of the Boy Scouts. It was not because of the prank on Mr. Dunwell; instead, it had to do with many other things that we had done over time. The troop just felt that it would be in everyone's best interest, if we three were no longer involved with that Boy Scout troop.

Many years later, on three different occasions when I was in the Air Force, I came very close to being tossed out of that organization as well. I can now understand that I may have always harbored resentment toward authority and uniforms.

Eight

We de'peed Manny and No-Nose on Schiller Park's Round Top. Axle wanted to get back at the two brothers for everything they had ever done to him. De-panting the Winkle brothers was a way that Axle could get even. But, it was not a planned event; the de-panting of Manny and No-Nose just happened. It happened after a touch football game.

Schiller Park, on the north side of Syracuse, was a place the Northsiders used quite a bit. During the summer months, we could swim in the old concrete pool, or play basketball at one of the two basketball courts. There were two baseball fields and two tennis courts also.

The Round Top was a large hill located at the top of the park. It had a view overlooking the North Side. There was a flat area on which we used to play touch or tackle football. The road up the Round Top was a popular parking place when couples wanted to make out in their cars.

On the summer day when we de'peed Manny and No-Nose, Schiller Park was filled with young children and their parents. All of the Back Alley Boys, along with many other Northsiders, were there. We played tackle football on the Round Top, and when the game ended, a few of the boys decided to go swimming down at the pool. Some of the others decided to play basketball. But, Axle, Shooter and I headed toward a small grocery store across from one of the Park entrances. As we walked down the hill, we noticed Manny and No-Nose walking in front of us. Axle decided to de-pant the brothers.

"Guys," Axle whispered. "Let's de'pee the faggots."

"Great idea," Shooter said as he rubbed his hands together in anticipation.

"You guys grab No-Nose. I'll take Manny myself," Axle whispered, pointing to a secluded area that was filled with large shrubs and a hedgerow of evergreens surrounded by old towering oaks about fifteen yards from us. We knew what Axle wanted us to do.

"When I say go," Axle whispered.

Manny and No-Nose knew that we were following them, but they were not paying attention. They were tired from all the running around they had done during the football game. Although they never tackled anyone, or ever ran with the ball, they still managed to become fatigued. We figured the Winkles became tired because they spent all of their time running away from the contact on a play. They were very good at managing to be at the wrong end of the action.

When Axle yelled, "Go," we grabbed the Winkle brothers. They were caught completely off-guard. While they kicked and screamed, we dragged them toward the hedgerow. Axle held Manny in a bear hug and carried him into the shrubs. Shooter and I carried No-Nose by his feet and arms. They both continued to scream and then Axle told the brothers to shut up, or he would stuff their socks into their mouths. When we had the two brothers on the ground, Axle sat on Manny's chest, and Shooter sat on No-Nose's.

"What you guys doin'?" Manny asked. He was scared. No-Nose started to cry.

"Stop cryin' you sissy." Axle told him. "We're not gonna hurt you."

Manny tried to get up, but Axle's weight kept him down.

"We didn't do nothin' to you," Manny pleaded.

"This is for all the times before, creep. Stretch? Change places with me."

I moved over to where Manny was lying and sat on top of him. Axle began to unbuckle Manny's belt. The Crout shook his hips and kicked his legs. No-Nose was still crying and was begging Axle to leave his brother and him alone.

"Ppplease, Ax. We'll be good from now on," he cried.

"Both of you shut up or I'll stuff a sock in it," Axle said.

Manny continued to kick as Axle struggled to pull his pants off. When he finally removed them, Axle went after Manny's underwear. Manny screamed and Axle put his hand over his mouth.

"Okay I warned you."

"Stretch. Hold his arms."

Manny was weak, so I had no problem grabbing his hands and sitting on them, as they pressed against his chest. Axle removed Manny's sock and stuffed it into his mouth.

No-Nose had stopped struggling. He knew it was hopeless, that he was losing the battle. His crying became a whimper as he watched Axle remove Manny's underwear. Axle threw the underwear on the ground next to where Manny's pants lay.

"Oh wow, sissy. Manny ain't got any ball hairs," Axle said laughing.

"Look at his tiny weenie," Shooter laughed.

Manny tried to talk, but the sock was stuffed too far into his mouth. He finally stopped kicking and lay still on the ground.

No-Nose watched Axle approach him. He knew he was next.

I continued to sit on Manny's arms and chest, and while Shooter sat on No-Nose. Axle removed his pants and underwear.

"He's hairless too," Axle said. "Come on, let's go."

Quickly, we picked up the Winkles' pants and underwear. We carried them away with us and left the two brothers alone, butt-naked from the waste down and wondering how they were going to get home.

We were hungry and thirsty, so we stopped at the grocery store across from the Schiller Park. Each of us bought a bottle of Ma's Cola and a Hostess Twinkie. We had a long walk home.

Nine

I never had a steady girlfriend while in junior high or high school. There were a few girls that I was interested in. However, because I was with Axle so much, I never had time to date. Axle never had a steady girlfriend until his senior year. That relationship did not last long. Axle was too much of a show-off, and girls thought he was arrogant. After a while, his attitude rubbed girls the wrong way. He tried too hard to be cool. That was his downfall.

Shooter was different. He always had a girlfriend. He was good-looking and that helped. He was also the star baseball, football, and basketball player in school. He attracted girls like a magnet. Shooter liked to brag about his sexual encounters. Whether his stories were true was always in question. Nevertheless, his stories about his sexual exploits were exciting to listen to. As Shooter and I walked from the North High School baseball field one summer day, he was determined that I hear about his latest episode with the opposite sex.

"Stretch? I was with No Panty Annie last night," Shooter said as he pumped his fists into the air.

"Wow, she's ugly, but what a set of thumpers."

No Panty Annie was, in fact, a very ugly girl. Axle used to say that "she had a face like a torn sneaker." She was short and stumpy. Her hair was long and black and hung down to the middle of her back. And her breasts were extremely large for her age. No Panty Annie always wore mini skirts and would sit at her desk with her legs open. She never wore panties. We'd all heard the stories about Annie's sexual escapades, so, when Shooter told me his story, I listened with excitement.

"She loves it, Stretch," Shooter said. He was pumping his arms in front of his hips, demonstrating the act of intercourse.

"We were walking from school. And she asks me if I wanna take her up to Gilbert Hill. So when we get up there, she throws me into the bushes. Then she starts to take her blouse off. And while she's doing that she tells me to take out my boner."

Shooter was jumping all around, still pumping his fists in the air, and making circular motions with his hips.

"As soon as I seen her thumpers, I couldn't resist. I put the bone to her right there in the bushes, Stretch. It was great."

I never knew what to say to Shooter after he described his sexual encounters. I was sure that any questions I asked Shooter would get an exaggerated answer.

"I had to buy her a bottle of Ma's Cola when we finished," he said "But it was worth it. She'll do anything for a Ma's Cola."

"Hey Stretch. You got any yet?"

We had just reached my home at the end of Back Alley.

"Shooter, I'm not as lucky as you are," I said with envious disappointment.

"Hey, your day is coming," Shooter remarked. He walked away from my front yard. He was still pumping his fists in the air and screaming, "All you need is a bottle of Ma's Cola."

I was jealous of Shooter. Even though I was not sure if his stories were true, I had wished that they were real. I wanted to believe that it was possible for a ninth grader to have sexual intercourse. If it were true, then there was still hope for Axle and me.

The summer of 1962 was a summer of anticipation. I would be entering high school as a sophomore in the fall. I was excited. Going to high school meant that I was a mature young man. It meant that I would be looked up to by all of the younger kids in the neighborhood. Also, becoming a sophomore in high school brought with it certain perks. Since my neighborhood friends and I were to be tenth graders, we could look forward to hanging out with the junior and senior class of the high school. It meant that we could date older women like the seniors. In the summer of 1962, for the first time, I was actually looking forward to starting another school year.

Years before, the name Windy Hillers had been given to the students who attended North High School. The name Windy Hiller was synonymous with the term Northsider. You were proud to wear the school colors of maroon and white. However, in 1963, North High School was to cease to exist. It would become just another piece of North Side history. We would become the last students to walk the halls of old North High. In the following year, the Northsiders would merge with the students of Eastwood, whose school was also closing, and begin our studies at the new Henninger High School.

By the time my parents had attended North High School in the 30s, the school already had history attached to it. North High had not always been a school. It had started out as a penitentiary during the middle 1800s. My grandfather had worked as a guard at the prison, and I can remember staying up late at night listening to his prison stories. My favorite stories were about the escape attempts and how the prison was haunted.

My grandfather told me he'd seen a headless prisoner walking the halls of the prison late at night. The headless man, according to Grandpa, had been a prisoner for many years. Everyone had despised the man because he'd been a troublemaker for the other inmates and the guards. The headless prisoner was Leonard Gippy. Everyone called him Gippy. Gippy was in prison for murdering his own mother. According to Gramps, Gippy had stabbed her because she'd over cooked his steak. After murdering his mother, he'd cut her into little pieces and, except for her head, had hid her body parts in the basement of their home. Grandpa said that Gippy had attached his mother's head to the front door for everyone to see. When Gippy was put into the prison, everyone, including prisoners who were murderers themselves, hated him for killing his own mother, especially the way that he'd done it.

One day, two guards discovered Gippy's severed head hanging from his cell door. They never found his body, nor did they ever find out who'd killed him. It was a strange murder. And, almost as strange were the sightings of Gippy after his death. Grandpa said that prisoners, as well as guards, used to see the figure of a headless person moving around the prison. Gramps told me he'd seen Gippy on two different occasions. One time when he was working late at night and checking the cells, he'd felt someone standing behind him. When he turned around, he saw the silhouette of a headless figure walking toward him. Grampa told me he never did finish checking the prisoners' cells that evening.

There were also stories of neighbors near the prison seeing a headless figure. My grandfather told me that Mr. Jacobs, who used to live next to us, was awakened from his sleep by a noise coming from his kitchen. When he went to investigate, he saw a ghostly figure standing in front of him. The ghost was headless, that was the way Gramps explained it to me.

Ten

I tried to be a good Catholic son. However, it was a standard that was difficult to live up to, especially when I was with Axle. If my mother and father had ever found out what we had done one particular Sunday morning, they would have grounded me for a year.

It was a typical Sunday morning, and like other good Italian Catholic children, I was preparing to go to church. Anyway, that was what my parents thought I was doing. At age eleven, I felt I'd had enough of church and religion. Besides, I thought, church isn't helping me anyway—I was still getting into trouble and skipping school. So, I decided to abandon the idea of going to church on Sundays. In addition, sitting in church and listening to a boring priest talk about things that didn't make sense to me was the last thing I wanted to do. Although I believed in God and prayed often, I figured that was enough. So, just like school, I would skip church. I would meet Axle at his home and then we would walk toward the large Catholic church, giving the impression that we were going, while in reality, on most Sundays, Axle and I were going to hang out in Brown's Drug Store across the street from the church. We would stay there drinking malts and looking at girlie magazines. Then I would go home and tell my mother and father how nice the sermon had been. But, one Sunday morning, Axle came up with a different plan.

Like always on Sunday, we were dressed in our Sunday church clothes. We were walking in the direction of the church when Axle asked me a question.

"Stretch, you wanna pass on the malts this morning and drink some wine instead?"

"What you are talking about?" I asked.

"I know where they keep the wine for mass and we can get some real easy."

We reached the side entrance to the church. Many of the neighborhood families were gathering outside the door. There were fifteen minutes before the mass would be starting. Usually at this time, Axle and I would walk past the side door of the church and across the street to the drugstore. Instead, Axle grabbed my arm and pulled me around the corner of the church to the back door.

"Axle, you're nuts."

"Come on, Stretch. Grow some balls."

I knew it was wrong, but Axle had a way of convincing me to go along with just about anything he wanted to do.

"You don't even know where the wine is," I said to him.

"Yea I do. Scurvy Sam told me where the priests hide their stash. Follow me."

Without warning, I was pulled into the back entrance of the church.

"Be quiet," Axle whispered. I followed him slowly down a set of steep stairs.

At the bottom of the stairs was a long hallway. On each side of the hallway were rooms; some of them had their doors open. Reluctantly, I followed Axle to each door; he was searching for one in particular. My heart was racing and I kept looking over my shoulder to see if anyone had spotted us. Axle kept walking as if he was taking a stroll in the park.

"Here it is," he whispered. I followed him toward the door. The door was closed, but it was unlocked. The small brass sign on the door read, "RECTORY." Axle walked into the room. I continued to follow him. It was a very large room with doors on each side. My heart was racing as I followed Axle to each door where he would stop just long enough to read its brass sign. He didn't seem to care about being caught by one of the priests. Suddenly, he stopped at a door that had a sign that read, "SUPPLY ROOM." Axle slowly turned the doorknob and went in.

"You thirsty, Stretch?" Axle asked as I followed him. We closed the door behind us.

"Ax, we gotta get out of here," I urged him. My palms were sweaty and my heart felt as though it were going to jump from my chest.

"No way, Stretch. We're too close. Scurvy said the vino is supposed to be in that cabinet."

Axle pointed to a large tall metal cabinet. It stood against the far wall.

"That's gotta be it," he whispered.

Axle ran across to the metal cabinet and opened its two doors. On the first two shelves were a dozen bottles of red wine.

"Wow! Thank you, Jesus," Axle said as he reached for a bottle of wine.

"Look at this stash, Stretch. We're in heaven."

"Come on Ax, let's get out of here. I have a bad feeling about this."

"Not so fast, pal. Look at this," he said, looking in the cabinet. "They made it easy for us. Here's a corkscrew to open the bottles."

Axle sat down in the corner of the rectory next to the metal cabinet. Leaning back against the wall, he began uncorking the bottle.

"Let's take it with us, Axle," I urged.

"First, I gotta get a swig of this stuff," he replied.

Axle managed to wrestle the cork from the bottle. He put the bottle to his lips and gulped down three huge tastes of the red nectar.

"Oh, this is good stuff. Here Stretch. Take some." He handed me the bottle.

Reluctantly, I sipped the wine. It had a dry, pungent taste, unlike my grandfather's wine, but I drank it anyway.

After a few minutes of handing the bottle of wine back and forth between us, I found myself becoming less concerned about being caught. Axle and I began to speak in loud whispers.

"Hey Stretch," Axle burped, "you wanna bless me?" He was laughing and slapping his legs.

"Sure Ax, I'll bless you." I took another long gulp of wine.

I stood up and put my hands on Axle's forehead.

"I bless thou, Axle." Hiccup. "And may he graduate. Someday." Hiccup. "And become President." Hiccup.

I sat down next to Axle. We laughed hysterically and sat in the corner, not caring that just above us a Sunday Mass was being held. We didn't care if a priest caught us drinking the wine. Axle and I had no cares at all that Sunday morning. Our only concern was how many bottles of wine we could consume while the church services were being conducted. I finally confessed to Axle that it was better than hanging out at Brown's Drugstore and drinking malts.

After a while, I stood up, realizing that we needed to get out because mass would soon be over. I felt the inside of my head spin around in circles. I had to lean against the wall or else I would have fallen over. Axle stood up and started laughing, but he was dizzy too. He sat down again.

"Geez, Stretch," hiccup, "I'm drunk," he said laughing.

"Shit. My legs feel wike wubber. I mean rubber." We both laughed at how we were talking. The harder we tried to talk correctly, the more drunk we sounded.

"We're drunk as sailors," Axle said as he tried to stand up.

I finally managed to stand without leaning against the wall, but wobbled unsteadily.

"We gotta get outta," hiccup, "here, Ax," I managed to say.

"Yea sure. I'm," hiccup, "blessed enough for taday."

Axle stood up slowly. He started to walk across the room and bumped into a stack of boxes, knocking them over.

"Ooh sshit, SStretch." Axle burped again. "I'm drunker than you are." Hiccup! "I'mm . . . drunker 'n a skunk. I'm a drunker 'n a sailor."

I grabbed Axle's arm and walked him out the door. We leaned on each other, trying to steady one another. My legs would not react to what my brain was telling them to do. Somehow, we managed to walk up the staircase and out to the street. There were still a few minutes left before the church services would be over. Axle and I were still holding onto each other when we stumbled past the church entrance. We started praying for the first time that Sunday, hoping that no one would see us. I especially did not want my brother Rich or my sister Kathleen to see me drunk. They would have loved to tell my parents what I had done.

"AAAxle we can't ga hhome now. We're drunk," I said, burping up bitter wine.

"Jist kkeep wa . . . walkin' cause . . . ," hiccup, "ca … cause if we gonna stop," hiccup, "we'll faw down," Axle replied.

We managed to walk a few blocks from the church in the opposite direction of our homes. We were not sure where we were going. We just knew that home was not the best place to be at that moment.

"Hey SStretch? Less go to SSSkeleton IIIsland."

"Oooh. Thas a ggood idea," I mumbled.

"Ya know, SStretch? I don't ffeel bblessed anymore. Da you?"

"Uhuh. I'm jist feelin' sick, AAxle."

Axle and I staggered our way to our hideaway. When we arrived at Skeleton Island, we laid down beneath the first large oak tree we came to. Within minutes, both of us had fallen asleep.

A few hours later, Axle and I woke from our deep sleep. We both had very bad headaches.

"Oooh damn, my head's pounding, Stretch." Axle was sitting up with both of his hands holding the sides of his head.

"Stretch, my brain feels like it's gonna explode. Does yours hurt?"

"Yes, thanks to you."

"I didn't twist your arm, ya know."

I tried to stand up but had to sit back down. I was still too dizzy to attempt standing. Axle did manage to stand. He was still holding the sides of his head.

"Have you got your watch, Stretch? What time is it?"

I glanced at my wristwatch. It was 3 p.m.; we had been gone for six hours. Axle and I were supposed to go to the 9 a.m. mass and then go immediately home afterwards. We needed to get home soon, and we needed to have an excuse as to why we were late.

On our walk home, we decided to tell our parents that we had gone to Skeleton Island after church because we thought it would be okay with them. One problem was that when we'd left home for church that morning we were neat and clean. But after consuming a bottle of wine and then sleeping on the ground for two hours, we were a mess. Our pants were dirty and our shoes were caked with mud. Our ties were wrinkled and our shirts hung outside of our pants. This was how we looked when we walked into our homes that Sunday afternoon.

But, we never gave a thought to how bad we looked. We just told our parents we were sorry, and that it would never happen again. Of course, it did happen again. But, although Axle and I continued to skip church every Sunday, we never drank the church wine again, nor did we want to. My mother would always ask me how the mass went, and I would tell her it was very uplifting.

My mother also expected me to go to confession. However, I believed I had confessed enough sins already in my young life. I believed that going to confession was a waste of time. So, after a while, I even lied to my mother about going to confession. I had better things to do.

However, when I did go to confession, I made a game out of it. I would make up lies in the confessional booth, telling the priest stories I would make up as I went along. I had gotten that idea from Axle. He'd told me how he would make up stories in the confessional booth.

Soon, Axle and I began to play a game of "who can come up with the best lies during confession." The person who received the most "Hail Marys" and "Our Fathers" as punishment was the winner. Axle held the record with forty Hail Marys and forty Our Fathers. But one day I came close to beating him.

I had been arguing with my mother about going to confession. She told me that if I did not go, she would make me trim the hedges and sweep our long driveway. I finally gave in after she told me that she would tell my father about our argument. I was angry as I walked to church. My intentions were to take out my frustrations on the priest. I went into the dark, closet-sized confessional booth and knelt down. Within a few seconds, the voice on the other side of the wall told me to begin.

"Bless me, Father, for I have sinned."

"Begin."

"Well Father, . . . uhh . . . I've had bad thoughts."

"Oh. What kind of thoughts?"

"Well . . . uhh."

"Go ahead. Remember, God will forgive you."

"Father . . . uhh . . . I have been thinking about boinking the girls at school."

Tightly, I covered my mouth with both hands. I did not want him to hear me laughing.

"What do you mean by boinking?"

"You know, Father? Doing it to her."

"Oh. I see." The Father cleared his throat. "And how often do you have these thoughts, my son?"

"All day long, Father."

"Hmm. Every hour?"

"Every hour. Day and night."

My side was hurting from holding in my laughter.

"You do recognize that those thoughts are sinful, don't you?"

"Yes, Father. That's why I'm here."

"That is a fine beginning to your confessions to God, my son. Is there anything else you would like to confess?"

"Well . . . uhh . . . yes, Father."

"Go on."

"There are a few teachers that I think about boinking also."

"How many teachers do you think about?"

"Three, Father."

"Three? And are these thoughts everyday?"

"Oh yes, Father."

I heard the Father clear his throat.

"And do you recognize that these impure thoughts are a sin?"

"Yes, Father. That's why I'm here."

"That is good, my son. God will absolve you of your sins. Is there anything else?"

"Yes, Father."

I was squeezing both of my hands tightly over my mouth to keep my laughter inside. I was not sure how much longer I could continue lying to the priest.

"Okay continue." There was tension in his voice.

"Well, Father . . . I . . . uh."

"Go on."

"I . . . ugh . . . touch myself."

"You do?"

"Yes."

"Where do you touch yourself?"

"You know. Down there?"

"How many times a day?"

"How many times a day what, Father?"

The priest was becoming more annoyed with me.

"How many times a day do you touch yourself down there?"

I took a deep breath.

"Umm . . . eight or nine times a day." I could hardly contain myself from laughing.

The Father hesitated for a moment. I could tell that he was giving some thought to my confession.

"And do you know that touching yourself down there is a sin?"

"Yes I do, Father. That's why I'm here."

"Then God will forgive you for your sins. Now. Is there anything else you want to tell me?"

I figured he'd had enough, so I told him I was through. Besides, I knew I had Axle's record beaten with this confession. But, the Father only gave me a penance of twenty-five Hail Marys and twenty-five Our Fathers. I couldn't believe it. I walked from the confessional wondering to myself, what did I have to confess to if I wanted to break Axle's record of forty Hail Marys and forty Our Fathers. All of my lying to the priest and it had only gotten me twenty-five and twenty-five. Dejected, I kneeled at the altar and began saying my penance of Hail Marys and Our Fathers. I said the prayers as fast as I could. I even lost count. I wanted to get out and meet up with Axle. We were going fishing at Crap Lake.

Eleven

Tenth grade at North High School was a memorable one. It wasn't because my grades soared to new heights. Instead, it was a year to be remembered because of how we, the students, treated poor old North. North High School was finally closing its doors forever, and the students could not have cared less how they treated her. Nor did we care about how we treated some of the teachers and our principal.

It was a common occurrence to see the old wooden desks being thrown from the school windows. Even during class, it was not unusual to see a desk go tumbling by outside. That is what happened in Mr. Garrison's class one day. Some of the students were preparing to toss a desk out of his classroom window and he demanded that they "stop the carnage" or they would be turned over to Mr. Peel, the principal. But, the students hated Mr. Garrison and Mr. Peel. So, they threatened to hang both of them from the classroom window.

Arthur Garrison was a science teacher and an autocrat. He did not teach his classes; he ruled them. He was loud and belligerent and continually belittled his students. Mr. Garrison had a mean looking face; it fit his character perfectly. Most of the students would rather have had all of their teeth pulled without a painkiller than to sit in one of Mr. Garrison's classes. A rumor had circulated for years that his children and wife had hated him so much that they'd left him years earlier.

My first experience with Mr. Garrison was not a pleasant one. In the tenth grade, I was unfortunate enough to have him for my first period science class. Mr. Garrison had a routine on the first day of every new school year. He would tell each one of his new students to stand in front of the class and say their name. Then he would check the name against the list of students who were supposed to be present.

I was nervous because I had heard about how mean he was. Mr. Garrison sat behind his desk like a judge in a courtroom. When it was my turn to stand, I wanted to make sure that I said my name loud enough for him to hear.

Poor fat Willie Koegel was also one of the unfortunates. Willie was a nervous kid, who was fat and sloppy. When it was his turn to stand up and say his name, he became stuck in his seat. The old inkwell-type desk was just not wide enough for fat Willie. As he struggled to stand, Mr. Garrison became enraged and screamed, "WHAT IS THE MATTER WITH YOU, SON? I TOLD YOU TO STAND UP AND SAY YOUR NAME."

The harder fat Willie tried to stand, the more nervous he became. And, the more nervous he became, the harder it was for him to free himself from his desk. We started to laugh and Mr. Garrison put a quick stop to that.

"Son?" Mr. Garrison stood up. He had a mean look on his face.

"If you do not tell me your name, I will personally come over there and MAKE YOU TELL ME!" he screamed.

That was all Willie could handle. The pressure was too much, and he began to mumble something. Poor Willie was stammering and wrestling with the seat at the same time.

Mr. Garrison had had enough. He walked over and grabbed Willie's ear, yanking him from his desk. Then, leading Willy by his ear, he walked him to a closet in the back of the room. Mr. Garrison forced fat Willie into the closet and then closed the door.

"Can you hear me, son?" he asked through the closet door.

Willie's voice was shaking and barely audible. "Yes."

"You are already in trouble, son." The veins in Mr. Garrison's forehead were popping out.

"I know," Willie whispered.

"Then do not answer me with just 'yes.' Do you remember how to address me?"

"Yes, sir!" Willie yelled out from behind the closet door.

"Good boy. Maybe we are making progress with you. Now son, when you can remember your name, I want you to knock on this door. And then, when I ask you 'what does the boy in the closet want?', I would like you to tell me your name. Do you think you can do that?"

"But I already know my name, sir," Willie answered.

"No, son. I want you to think about your name over and over. I want you to never forget what your name is. I want you to make sure you always get your name right. Do you understand?"

"Yes, sir."

"Good. Now you just wait and think about your name for a few more minutes. IS THAT UNDERSTOOD?" Mr. Garrison screamed.

The class heard Willie whisper, "Okay, I mean, yes, sir."

Mr. Garrison walked back to his desk and sat down.

"Who's next?" he asked, while trying to regain his composure.

It was my turn to stand in front of my new classmates. No problem, I thought, I know my name. I stood up, and bravely looked Mr. Garrison right in his eyes. Confidently, I said my name.

"Frank Pandozzi, sir."

Mr. Garrison looked down at his class list and then up at me. Again, he looked mean. Mr. Garrison asked me once again what my name was, and again I told him.

"My name is Frank Pandozzi, sir."

Mr. Garrison's veins looked like they were about to explode from his forehead and temples. They were ready to burst from all the pressure that was building up inside of them. He stared at me a long time. It seemed like hours. I tried to look at the floor, but every time I did, he told me to look at him.

"You have one more chance to give me your correct name or you will be joining your classmate in the closet."

As Mr. Garrison was talking, we could hear Willie knocking on the door from inside the closet. "Mr. Garrison, sir, I know my name now."

He kept staring at me. The anger in his face was frightening, and I was not sure why.

"Shut up in there!" he yelled to fat Willie. "I AM NOT READY FOR YOU JUST YET."

Mr. Garrison walked from behind his desk and approached me. I could see his neck veins; they were pulsating with each beat of his angry heart. He stepped right up into my face.

"You are not Frank Pandozzi are you?" he asked.

I thought for a moment.

"Sir, I was Frank Pandozzi when I got up this morning."

My classmates laughed, but I was not trying to be funny. I'd answered him truthfully.

He yelled at the class and told them that they were already on his bad side, and they'd better keep their mouths shut.

"Let me help you to remember who you are. I am going to ask you a question."

"Sure, sir."

"Are you Francis Pandozzi?"

I suddenly felt my heart slip into my stomach. Beads of perspiration formed on my face. I began to feel weak and sick to my stomach. I wanted to run from the school and hide. Maybe I would go to Skeleton Island. There, I would become a recluse and live off the land. I did not need school, I thought, or Mr. Garrison. With that one question, my life had changed. From that day forward, everyone would frown upon me. My life was over. I would never again be able to face my friends or my classmates.

"I asked you a question. Are you Francis Pandozzi?"

I could taste the bile that had moved up from my stomach. I gathered my courage, and in a soft whisper, I answered, "Yes, sir."

He was standing with his face just inches from mine. I could smell his garlic breath and he nauseated me.

"THEN TELL ME YOUR NAME, SON. SAY IT SO I CAN HEAR YOU?"

"Francis Pandozzi, sir." I was embarrassed as I yelled out my name. I could hear the giggles from my classmates. I wanted to run into the closet and hide with fat Willie, who was still pounding on the closet door.

I hated that name. I never used it. As far as I was concerned, Francis was a girl's name. I never forgave my parents for giving me that sissy name. To this day, I am still surprised that my tough marine father would have allowed his son to be named Francis. I asked my mother once, "Why was I named after a mule?" She never answered me.

From that day forward, Mr. Garrison called me Francis. So did many of my friends and classmates. I hated Mr. Garrison for that, and I vowed to get back at him for embarrassing me in class.

In contrast to Mr. Garrison's tyrannical, egomaniacal persona, Mr. Peel, the principal at North, was a milksop. He was a coward who never stood up for his students. If there was a disagreement between a student and a teacher and it escalated to Mr. Peel's office, then the teacher, in Mr. Peel's eyes, was always right. Even when the teacher was wrong in Mr. Peel's eyes, the student was always wrong. Mr. Peel was always looking for a way to impress his teachers as well as the school administrators. The students of North High resented that, and they had just as much contempt for Mr. Peel as they had for Mr. Garrison. It was that contempt that led to a group of jocks to try to hang the two of them from a second floor classroom window.

It happened during exam week, the last week of school. By then, most of the furniture had been burned or thrown from the windows. The carnage had begun early in the school year. It was a common experience to be sitting outside the school during lunch, or a free class, and suddenly see a desk come sailing out of a window.

A few of the school jocks, along with Scams, who was a friend of one of them, had bought three bottles of cheap wine. They wanted to celebrate the end of the school year, and the closing of North High School. Joe Paluka was a three-year letterman in football. He was big, strong, and dumb. Many of us wondered what Joe Paluka's age really was. We figured he was probably in his mid-twenties, while his classmates were seventeen or eighteen years old. He had failed school so many times that it became difficult to figure his age. Paluka was a maniac. When he played football, he would tackle the opposing running back and then stand over him growling. If his opponent got up right away, Paluka would knock him back down. Of course, the refs were always blowing their whistles at Paluka for an unsportsmanlike conduct penalty, but he didn't care.

And, on the football field, Joe Paluka always referred to himself in the third person. He would say to the kid he'd just tackled, "You better stay down or Paluka's gonna knock your head off." Sometimes, he would tell his opponent that he would disfigure them if they got up from the ground too fast. His favorite line was, "Paluka's gonna tear your ass off and cover your head with it." Joe Paluka was not someone to mess with.

Paluka, Scams and two others, Anthony Stottmire and Casey Peterson, became drunk on the cheap wine. The four of them sat in Paluka's 1960 Chevy, which was parked in the school parking lot, and became drunk after consuming the three bottles of wine. After drinking the wine, the four drunken students decided it was payback time for the two people in the school they hated the most, Mr. Garrison and Mr. Peel.

It was early afternoon; most of the students had left the school. The four drunks, led by Paluka, walked into Mr. Garrison's room. The teacher was cleaning out his desk and filling his briefcase with papers. When he saw them enter his class, he acted the way he usually did—he screamed at them. He went into a rage and yelled at them for being there without permission. Hating Mr. Garrison as much as they did, and being filled with cheap wine, the four drunks became even more irritated.

Paluka approached Mr. Garrison and told him he'd had enough of his anger. Paluka told Stottmire and Peterson to go to Mr. Peel's office and tell him that he was needed in Mr. Garrison's classroom. He told them to make sure their request sounded urgent.

Mr. Garrison kept screaming at Paluka, telling him to get out of his classroom or he would make sure he never graduated. Paluka closed the classroom door and walked toward the teacher. He told Mr. Garrison he did not care about school. He ordered him to sit down, or else he would throw him out of the open window. When Mr. Garrison refused to sit, Paluka grabbed him by the shirt and dragged him to the window. Scams, who was watching the unfolding events, began to panic. This was not what he wanted to do. As he turned to leave, Anthony Stottmire and Casey Peterson returned with Mr. Peel. When they'd entered the room, Paluka ordered Stottmire to close the door. He told Scams to stand by the door, just in case someone tried to enter. But

Scams, who wanted no part of it, left and walked out of the school.

Paluka told Stottmire to watch the door. Mr. Peel was scared. He began shaking and asked the students what they were going to do. He tried to reason with them, telling them they would go to jail and that they would have a record that they would carry for a long time. However, the three students, especially Paluka, would not listen. Mr. Peel began to beg for forgiveness while Mr. Garrison yelled obscenities at the students. Once again, Paluka grabbed hold of Mr. Garrison's shirt.

"Howdaya like it, teach?" Paluka asked. He pushed Mr. Garrison toward the open window.

Mr. Garrison said nothing but struggled to get free. It was hopeless; Paluka was just too big and too strong.

"Anthony, grab his feet," Paluka told his friend.

"Casey, you watch the worm," Paluka said pointing to Mr. Peel.

Mr. Peel was sitting at Mr. Garrison's desk. He was crying.

"Look at the sissy principal," Paluka taunted. "You wanna Kleenex?" he asked sarcastically.

Mr. Peel begged them to stop. He watched in horror as Anthony Stottmire and Paluka picked Mr. Garrison up and hoisted him onto the edge of the third floor window.

Paluka held Mr. Garrison in a chokehold around his neck. Anthony Stottmire had the teacher by his legs.

"I want his feet, Anthony," Paluka said. "You hold onto him."

Paluka grabbed his feet and told him he was going to hang him upside down from the window and make him apologize for being an asshole of a teacher.

Mr. Garrison told Paluka that he was even more stupid than he'd thought, and that he would not apologize.

Mr. Peel was still crying. He begged Mr. Garrison to do as Paluka had asked. But again, Mr. Garrison refused to obey his pleas. In an instant, Paluka lifted Mr. Garrison by his feet and placed him on the window ledge. Mr. Garrison tried to break free of Paluka's grasp, but it was no use.

"You're gonna go out the window, teach. I hope you can fly," Paluka laughed.

Mr. Peel was still sobbing as he sat behind Mr. Garrison's desk. Paluka told Stottmire to grab Mr. Garrison around his waist. The teacher was still sitting on top of the window ledge. If he moved, Paluka told him, he would push him off the edge.

Stottmire did as he was told. He grabbed Mr. Garrison around his waist. Paluka took hold of the teacher's ankles and lifted him out of the open window. Just as Paluka was about to hold him upside down out the window, the classroom door opened. Scams and two policemen walked into the room. With them was Mr. Grabowski, a school administrator.

Mr. Garrison was pulled back into the room by the two policeman. Mr. Peel was still sobbing as Mr. Grabowski consoled him. The three students were taken away to the city police station, arrested and placed in jail. They were later suspended from school for the following year. That meant that Joe Paluka, who was a senior, would not be graduating from North High School that year. He ended up quitting school anyway and joined the Army. He went to Vietnam and then went AWOL; Joe Paluka was never heard from again.

Mr. Garrison and Mr. Peel had had enough of school. Although they had positions waiting for them at other schools, they both decided that it was time to retire. The incident with Joe Paluka had something to do with their decisions. They both retired on the last day of school.

Twelve

When the school finally closed its doors, it passed into history without celebration.

Yet, even though North High had closed its doors to future generations of students, its baseball field was still used by the Northsiders. But, baseball was not the only game played on North's field. Touch and tackle football were also played. The football games were played mostly during the fall when the regular college and pro football season started. This was also the time when the Northsiders felt like throwing themselves at each other like their heroes on the major gridirons. Many bones were broken on North's ball field. We played tackle football without the aid of shoulder pads or football helmets. There was never a day when a tackle football game did not result in a broken collarbone, arm, or leg. Chipped teeth, sprained ankles, and broken noses were a common occurrence during the games, but we continued to play anyway. And, it was not just at North High where we played touch football; we played anywhere on the North Side where there was a park. During the fall months and into early winter, someone always carried a football with them.

One day I initiated a startup game of touch football. The game almost ended my short life. It was in the early fall of my junior year at Henninger High. It was a Saturday, and Axle and I were lying around his house watching the Saturday morning cartoons. Bugs Bunny and Popeye were our favorites. We never missed a Saturday morning in front of the TV unless we were going fishing or hanging out at Skeleton Island. Axle was sprawled out on the sofa and had just finished his third bowl of cheerios. I was lying on the floor.

"Let's go toss the football around," I said.

"Yea. Good idea," Axle replied as he stretched his arms. "Just let me comb my hair."

"You and that hair. You're only gonna get it messed up anyways."

"Gotta look good all the time, Stretch," he said as he stood in front of the bathroom mirror, patting his hair in place.

When Axle finally finished manicuring his hair, he grabbed his football and we headed out the door.

"Hey Stretch, let's see if Scurvy's around. Maybe he'll wanna play."

Scurvy Sam lived about four blocks from Axle and me. Across the street from his house was a small park. After stopping at Scurvy's, the three of us went to the park and began to pass the football around.

"Go deep, Stretch!" Axle yelled to me.

At full throttle, I started to run away from him looking back over my shoulder. He threw me a perfect pass as I ran full speed. Still running, I caught the ball and immediately turned at full gallop. I do not remember running into the telephone pole. Nor do I remember falling to the ground. But, I do remember Scurvy and Axle looking down at me as I lay on the ground.

"Oh geez, Axle. He ain't movin'. Is he dead?"

"I think he's alive. I can see his chest move," I heard Axle say.

"Hey Stretch, say somethin'. It's me, Axle."

Everything around me was a blur. All I could do was moan. I was in pain from the meeting I'd just had with the telephone pole. I managed to hit it dead center, at full speed, right where the steel first step was located. My nose and my face began to throb, and my teeth felt separated from my gums. I could taste the blood as it pooled into my mouth.

"Damn. Look at his head, Axle. It's all swollen."

"Shut up, Scurvy. I see it."

"Hey Stretch, you gotta try to stand. Let's get you home," Axle said.

I couldn't stand. Everything that I focused on was spinning. I had to lie back down and wait for my head to clear, but it never did, at least not that day. Axle and Scurvy finally helped me to walk home. My mother was in the kitchen getting dinner ready when Axle opened the back door and helped me in.

"Oh my God! Oh sweet Jesus. Frankie? What happened? Quick sit down. You need ice on your head. Oh mother of God!" she screamed.

"Mrs. Pandozzi, look at his head," Scurvy remarked. "It's really big and swollen."

"Shut up, Scurv," I heard Axle say.

My father heard my mother screaming and walked into the kitchen. His response was typical.

"You stupid bastard. You have to mess around don't you. You know what this is gonna cost in doctor's bills?"

My sister Kathleen started to scream. She hated the sight of blood. My brother Richard laughed when he saw my swollen head and face. My sister Angela came into the kitchen praying for me on her rosary beads.

I was taken to the emergency room and given painkillers. I must have looked like a freak because everyone who saw me either laughed at my swollen head, or turned away in disgust. After a few x-rays and then meeting with a neurologist, I was sent home. Luckily, there were no broken bones or a concussion. My front teeth were permanently bent and I eventually needed root canals. I missed almost two months of school that year, which I did not mind.

It took that long for the swelling of my head and face to go away. I was the talk of the family for months. And, of course, being an Italian family, any story told between the older family members became dramatized and exaggerated. By the time the story of me running into a telephone pole reached my great aunts, I was in a coma and wearing a body cast. My mother received a telephone call from my Great Aunt Josephine who lived in Pennsylvania. Aunt Josephine was 89 years old.

"Lena? Howsa Francheska? Mama mia. I'ma so sorry hesa ina sooo mucha paina. When theya taka him offa traction?"

"Aunt Josephine, Frankie is not in traction. And he's in no pain anymore."

"Oh my Godda. He'sa deada?"

"No Aunt Josephine, Frankie is not dead."

"Oh mama mia. Thanka Godda. Aunta Maria tella me a telephona polea falla downa on a Francheska."

"No Aunt Josephine, Frankie did not have a telephone pole fall down on him. He ran into it."

Aunt Josephine, along with my other aunts, had said a mass for me. They sent me prayer cards containing money and baked me dozens of Italian cookies. They treated my accident as if it was my death. But, it would be a few weeks before I could eat the cookies. I had to sip liquid foods through a straw until my face muscles were able to function again. I was unable to chew, or talk.

Although I could not play football or participate in any athletic activities while my head and face were healing, I did participate in one game that the Northsiders were always ready to play, and that was pitching coins.

We pitched coins anywhere we thought we would not be caught. Our parents did not want us flipping away our allowance money. One place where we tossed coins was in the alley between an old brewery and a German barroom. The smoke-filled bar was named, Steigers. It was a local hangout for the older North Side German populace. Between the brewery and the beer garden, the smell of beer permeated through the alley.

Pitching coins was a game in which Shooter excelled. Even when he was younger, Shooter would win coins from the older kids. There were many times when Shooter had won so many coins his pockets jingled when he walked. But there was one night in particular when Shooter really was on a shooter's roll.

It was a fall evening just after my accident. Axle came to my house wanting to know if I wanted to walk to Steigers for a game of pitching coins. He said that Shooter would be there, along with Scurvy, Skidmarks, Baby Face and the two Winkle brothers, Manny the Crout and No-Nose. I told my mother and father I was going to Franklin Elementary School to watch some friends play dodge ball. I walked out of the house with the coins I had been saving for baseball cards. Axle and I stopped to get Scurvy at his house, and the three of us walked to the alley.

It was getting dark but we knew the lights from the old brewery and Steigers beer hall would illuminate the alley enough for us to see our game. When we arrived at the alley, No-Nose and Manny the Crout were already there. They were practicing their coin flips against the back wall of the brewery.

"Look who's here? The three musketeers," Manny said to his brother.

"Keep it up, Crout, and I'll tear your head from your shoulders and stick it in your ass," Axle replied. "You better have lots of money, Crout," he continued, "cause I'm gonna clean you out."

Within minutes, the rest of the group had arrived and started to line up at the tossing line. The line was drawn in white chalk on the ground. It was approximately twelve feet from the wall of the brewery. We had to stand behind the line when flipping our coins toward the wall. The closest coin to the wall was the winner, and the person who flipped their coin nearest the wall won all of the coins that had been previously tossed.

We started out by flipping our coins toward the wall to see who would go first. The closest coin to the wall had the option to flip first or last. Shooter always won the option and chose to go last. I could tell he would be tough to beat by his practice tosses. His technique for flipping coins was uncanny and perfected. Shooter would stand behind the tossing line with the coin resting on the tip of his right thumb and index finger. He would stand at the line and stare at the wall for what seemed like hours. His deliberate patience usually unnerved the others. It was a tactic that Shooter used to his advantage. After a few moments of staring down the wall, Shooter would very slowly swing his right arm high into the air, releasing his coin at just the right moment toward the wall. Most always, his coin would land just in front of the wall.

Axle flipped first. He stood crouched behind the tossing line with a nickel resting on his right thumb. He stared at the far wall, concentrating on his shot.

"Your mother wears combat boots," Manny suddenly screamed at Axle. No-Nose laughed at his brother's remark.

"Hey Axle, I hear that your mother has the clap," No-Nose yelled.

Axle ignored the Winkles' remarks. He knew their only way of winning this game was to try and upset the person tossing their coin.

Axle flipped his nickel toward the wall. The coin bounced lightly off the wall and landed approximately six inches away.

"Nice shot," Scurvy yelled. "I can beat it though. No sweat."

Scurvy stepped up to the line and flipped his nickel. It landed two feet short of the wall. Manny laughed and slapped his leg. No-Nose screamed, "You stink, Scurvy."

It was my turn next and my nickel bounced off the wall and landed a foot away. Then it was Skidmarks, Baby Face and Scams turns. Next came Shooter. He needed to beat Baby Face whose nickel had landed about two inches from the wall.

Shooter stood confidently behind the line, concentrating and staring at the wall. It was quiet until the Winkle brothers broke the silence.

"Your mother has a fat ass, Shooter," Manny laughed. "Wow, it's fat and ugly."

"Yea, she needs a license to carry it," No-Nose said laughing.

At any other time, Shooter never would have tolerated their remarks, nor would any of us, but this time was different. There was money at stake, and some of it belonged to the Winkles. Winning their money was more important than losing concentration by yelling back at them. And Shooter, in particular, would let no amount of harassment bother him.

Scams was different though. He walked over to Manny, grabbed his left ear, and twisted. At the same time, he took hold of the right ear of No-Nose and twisted it as well.

"I'll rip both your ears off if you don't shut up!" Scams yelled.

Instantly, the two brothers became quiet.

"I'm tired of listening to you guys," he continued to twist their ears. "Go ahead Shooter."

Shooter was still concentrating. There was $.50 in change, all nickels, lying on the ground in front of the wall.

When he was ready, he flipped his nickel from his high arching swing. The coin dropped perfectly against the wall, nestled between the wall and the ground. Shooter had won the first round of coins, but not before Boogers, who'd decided to show up to the game late, wanted a chance to win the first round. He walked into the alley just as Shooter was letting go of his coin.

"Mm-mm-my ta-turn," Boogers said while wiping the snot from his nose.

"Get lost freak," Manny yelled at him.

"Nn-nn-no. Ii-ii-ii-wa-wanna ta-turn."

"The game's over, Boogers. Come in the next one," Skidmarks told him.

"Ja-ja-jist le-le-let me-me-me sha-sh-shoot n-n-n-now. P-p-p-please."

"Hey freak, your nose is runnin' all over. Go catch it," Manny said laughing.

"Knock it off, Crout. Go ahead Boogers. Take a shot," Shooter told him.

"Tha-anks, Sha-Shooooter."

Boogers let go with a very high flip of his nickel. It hit the wall hard and bounced out on the ground approximately two feet from the wall.

"Not even close, dummy," Manny taunted.

"Hey Boogers, nice try," Shooter patted him on the shoulder and Boogers smiled back at him.

Shooter cleaned us out as usual. We left the alley around 10 p.m. and walked home. When I got home, my mother asked me how the dodge ball games had gone. I told her how difficult it was for me to just sit watching the game and not being able to play. My father never said anything. Nor did he even look my way. He was sitting on the couch smoking a Marlboro and watching Rawhide, one of his favorite TV shows.

    I walked by him to go into my room and he told me to be quiet. I lay down on my bed and turned on the radio to listen to the rock and roll station. I remember listening to Gene Pitney, Paul Anka, and The Supremes. I fell asleep dreaming about Tina.

    I was in love with Tina Battaglia, but Tina did not love me. She lived three blocks from Back Alley. She was the same age as I was. I started to watch Tina when we were both in the fourth grade when Tina first moved to the North Side from Italy. From the first moment I saw her, I knew I was in love. At least to the extent of what I thought love was. I had heard the word spoken within my family, and I thought I knew what love felt like between family members, but had never experienced what love was like outside my family. Tina changed that for me. She was the most beautiful girl I had ever seen.

    Tina moved from Italy to the North Side with her mother and father; they wanted a better way of life and to be with their family who had immigrated to the North Side a few years earlier. I was glad that Tina's family had moved to the North Side.

    Tina Battaglia's hair was black and shiny, like a polished ebony stone. It was long and flowed gracefully when she moved. She was tall for her age and very slender. Tina moved elegantly, like a dancer. Her face was angelic with a soft creaminess to it. It reminded me of a pure white flower blossom. She was Annette of the Mouseketeers.

    All the boys loved Annette, but Tina lived closer to me than Annette did, and I thought that perhaps someday I might have a better chance at marrying Tina. But, there was one problem. I never found the courage to talk to her even though I was in many of her classes. I became weak in my knees and began to sweat whenever I approached her to talk. At the last minute, just before I would start to form the words that I wanted to say, I would walk away. My shyness would turn into anger at myself for not having the courage to talk to her. So, I settled on the notion that I would have to be content just watching Tina and listening to her speak. I loved to hear her voice.

Tina had a beautiful voice. Her Italian accent was lovely and captivating. I wanted to record her voice and play it back whenever I felt alone or depressed. Tina's soothing voice was like a tonic that soothed me. Her face, her skin, her hair, her voice, those were the reasons why I loved Tina Battaglia. I'd only wished that Tina had loved me too.

Tina knew that I existed. She watched me watch her. She knew where I lived. She knew my friends, my teachers, my parents, but Tina did not know me. To her I was just another fourth grader, a person who lived a few blocks away from her. She must have known that I was shy. I wonder if she ever had thoughts about me.

Tina eventually moved away. I never found out where. I still become angry for not having had the courage to tell her how much I loved her. I often wondered if I had told her how I felt about her, what would she have said in return. Would she have laughed at me? Sometimes, when I am alone, my thoughts drift back to Tina Battaglia. Whatever happened to her? Is she happy? Does she have a family? Tina was an important part of my young life on the North Side.

Thirteen

My father was a tough ex-marine. He'd also spent time in the Army and had later joined the National Guard. He grew up on the streets of the North Side, tough and fearless, never backing down from anyone. Hour after hour, I would listen to his war stories. He told me about the time he was on Guadalcanal during WWII and how he had been blown out of his foxhole by an exploding mortar round. He told me about how he'd killed many Japs with his M1 rifle, and how he had to sleep in the rain and mud month after month. He talked about his recurring problems with malaria and jaundice and the death of friends who'd been killed in the war. He was a street tough guy, but not so tough or fearless that he didn't need to hide in a cave on Guadalcanal for three days because he'd been frightened of the constant death that was all around him.

I understood war as something that had happened in the past, far away from the North Side. War to me was a history class taught by my father. So, when the Vietnam war broke out in the 60s, it became just another war story to read about in the local newspapers. It was another war far removed from the North Side. It was a war to watch on the evening news. The Vietnam war was a war being fought in a country most people had never heard of, a country light years away from the North Side. The Northsiders never talked much about the Vietnam war. Why should we? We were young and carefree. We were too busy playing baseball or touch football, or getting into trouble. Besides, by the time we graduated we figured the little war in Vietnam would become just another history lesson. But this time I would learn about war from a teacher, and not my father.

My perception of the Vietnam war changed in 1963 when it introduced itself to the North Side. Danny Heinz was a Northsider. He lived three blocks from me and attended one of the Catholic schools on the North Side.

Danny never hung out with us; he ran with a group of kids from his school. Only occasionally would our paths cross, either through a ball game or just passing each other on the street. Danny was a tough guy, and a difficult person to get to know. He was a few years older than our gang, and he thought he was superior to everyone else. Danny was an only child; his father had died many years earlier. I remember my mother telling me that when Danny enlisted in the Army after graduation, his mother almost had a nervous breakdown. "Why would he do that?" was the question being asked among the Northsiders. One day in the summer of 1963, Danny had been a Northsider trying to figure out what to do with the rest of his life. And, by the end of that summer, he was suddenly in the Army and being shipped away to some far away country—a country that until a few years ago was unknown to all of us.

A few months after Danny Heinz was sent off to fight in Vietnam, the war moved even closer to the North Side. I found out from Axle what had happened. It was after school one day just before Christmas break. Axle and I were walking home from North High School.

"Stretch, you hear about Heinzie?"

"What about?"

"Man, it's all over school."

"What is?"

"Heinzie was killed in Vietnam."

I grabbed Axle's arm and pulled him toward me.

"Don't fool around," I yelled.

"Stretch, it's true. Heinzie was killed in Vietnam."

I remember feeling numb. I became frightened and confused. This war is not supposed to be coming to the North Side, I thought. How can Heinz be here one day and then become dead the next day in a country that is so far away. I thought back to my father's war stories and wondered if I would someday be talking to my children about a war that I had been involved in.

Those words, "Heinzie was killed in Vietnam," were spoken throughout the North Side over the next few weeks. From the day that I had first learned about Danny's death, the war in Vietnam became more real. It had moved closer to home. It was not just another war in a small country of peasants, who fought for the most rice. The war was not about stopping the threat of communism, as the politicians wanted us to believe. The Vietnam war had become more than any of that. It was about people. It was about lives, young American lives that never had a chance to understand why they were fighting.

It also became a personal war. I needed to know why this tragedy had happened to Danny. My father had fought in WWII because the Japanese were a threat to the United States, especially after the bombing of Pearl Harbor. But Vietnam? What threat to the United States did that country pose? What threat were the Vietnamese to the Northsiders? And, why would Danny Heinz enlist in the Army knowing that he had a chance of being sent to Vietnam? Was it to prove how tough he was? Heinzie always had to portray the tough guy image. I could feel the war becoming personal. Would I have to enlist some day? Would I have to fight in the same absurd war that Heinzie had fought in? I thought about my North Side friends. How many of them would go to that war? And, how many would come back to the North Side alive? These questions haunted me for a very long time.

But, when you are young, you are resilient. You can bounce back from tragedy much quicker than when you are older. So, after a few weeks, the Vietnam war was tucked away into a deeper part of me. Of course, it had never really disappeared. When I played touch football, I would hear those words, "Heinzie was killed in Vietnam." In my room, or while tossing coins, the words, "Heinzie was killed in Vietnam," would come back to me. And now, years later, I can still hear those words: "Heinzie was killed in Vietnam."

Fourteen

In 1964, my North Side friends began to reach the age to drive cars. The age of sixteen was a kind of rite to passage, as it is today; when you're sixteen the whole world opens up to you. You can drive on a date, drive to school, to baseball games and to church. You can drive your parents to the A&P supermarket, or to a doctor's appointment, or you can just drive to show off. Driving was cool and you wanted to be seen behind the wheel of a car, especially if the car was yours.

Axle and I turned sixteen late in our junior year at Henninger High School. However, some of our North Side friends were six months to a year older than we were, so Axle and I had the opportunity to cruise the streets with them until we turned sixteen. Some of them, like Shooter and Scams and Manny the Crout, had already purchased their own cars. Most of us worked part-time jobs after school and weekends and had saved enough money to buy our first cars. When you owned your own vehicle, you were real cool, especially to the girls.

Shooter owned a 1958 Chevrolet. It used to belong to his father. It was white with a light blue interior and was very clean. As soon as he bought the car from his father, he installed chrome-reversed wheels and a new muffler system that sounded like an explosion every time Shooter touched the gas pedal. Shooter had gotten two speeding tickets by the time he turned seventeen but continued to drive because his father knew a city judge.

We all believed that Shooter's father was in the Mafia. That was the rumor that went around. Of course, the rumor was never really proven, and when we asked Shooter about it he would joke and say things like, "Just be good to me, or else."

Scams owned a 1959 Pontiac Bonneville. It had a dull blue color and was filled with rust holes. Both the front and back fenders were so lose that Scams kept them tied to the grills with rope. The interior of the car was dirty and torn; the car always smelled of cigarettes. Scams smoked all the time. He tried to speed in his Bonneville but the car had a governor on it, installed by his father. If the device was removed, his father would cancel Scams's insurance and he would not be allowed to drive.

Manny the Crout owned a 1957 Oldsmobile. His car was red with white trim. Manny never let anyone ride with him except his brother No-Nose, not that we cared. Besides, Manny was a maniac when driving. Because of his bad driving, he was given the name, "Manny the Maniac." His Oldsmobile could have been a great advertisement for a junkyard. Because of all the accidents that he was involved in, Manny's Olds was falling apart. The doors were smashed in and they would not close properly. The car had no bumpers because they had fallen off during one of his accidents. On both sides, from the front to the rear tire, the Oldsmobile was badly damaged due to collisions with other vehicles. Manny also had a perversion for trying to run people over. He would say that he was just trying to scare us, but we knew better. Manny was crazy enough to hurt someone.

Cruising the streets of Syracuse at night was one of the rites of passage we enjoyed. We drove along the streets to pick up girls, to drag race with other cars, or to just drive around and burn gas. One summer night in 1964, I was at Axle's house helping him dismantle an old outboard motor he'd bought for a dollar. Axle had purchased the motor from an old man who lived around the corner from us. Axle planned to fix the motor and then purchase a small fishing boat so we could fish Onondaga and Oneida Lakes. The only problem was Axle knew nothing about repairing outboard motors, nor did he have a car to pull the boat with. But that was the way Axle approached his ideas. He never thought things out. Anyway, on this particular night, Scams drove into Axle's driveway in his '59 Pontiac. We were in the backyard where the parts to the outboard motor were lying everywhere. Scams pulled his car into the driveway just short of where Axle and I had laid the propeller down. We thought Scams was going to run us over. He had his window rolled down and started talking to us even before the car had come to a stop.

"It's time to pick up some brawds," Scams yelled.

"Let's do it," Axle said as he put away some of the tools he'd borrowed from his father's garage. He walked toward Scams's car combing his thick, greasy, black hair. "I feel like tonight's the night, boys."

"You wanna ride shotgun, Stretch?" Axle yelled as he opened the front passenger door.

"You mean I get to ride shotgun this time?"

"Doesn't matter where I sit tonight, guys. This is gonna be my lucky night," Axle said while fingering the curl of hair that hung down the middle of his forehead.

Scams drove up and down N. Salina Street, and Axle screamed to every pretty girl he saw.

"Hey sweetheart. You're beautiful. Wanna make out," he yelled to a girl walking down the street by herself.

"Get lost creep," she yelled back.

"You're doin' good, Ax," Scams said as he maneuvered the big Pontiac through the streets of Syracuse.

We stopped at a light on N. Salina Street and a 1963 Ford Thunderbird pulled up next to us. In the car with the driver were two girls. One of them sat in the front seat and the other sat in the back on the driver's side. The driver of the Thunderbird began revving his engine challenging Scams to a race.

"You're beautiful," Axle yelled across to the girl in the backseat. "Wanna make out?"

"Up yours, asshole!" the driver of the Thunderbird screamed back. He revved his engine even louder.

"I wasn't talkin' to you peckerhead," Axle yelled back.

"Knock it off, Ax," I told him.

"I'm gonna waste this guy," Scams said as the light turned green.

Both cars sped away from the intersection. The Thunderbird's tires squealed for two blocks as it pulled away from Scams's Pontiac.

"He's laughing at you, Scams," Axle said. "What a piece of shit this car is."

"Would you like to walk, Ax?"

"Geez Scams, just kiddin'."

We drove around the North Side for about an hour. Axle failed to pick up any girls, which was nothing new. Scams wanted to stop at the A&W drive-in restaurant; the restaurant was a popular meeting place for kids who drove. Cute girls wearing shorts or short skirts waited on the cars as they pulled into the parking lot. During the summer months, the A&W parking lot was filled with cars driven by kids from all over Syracuse. This night was no different.

Soon after we'd placed our order through the outside speaker system, a girl wearing an A&W mini-skirt and hat walked up to Scams's car. She was a petite blonde, with deep blue eyes.

"God, I'm in love," Axle chimed. He was leaning out the car window to get a better look at the girl.

"I'll take you instead of that burger, sweetheart."

The pretty blonde did what she was supposed to do and smiled at Axle. As she was adjusting the tray full of hamburgers, chilidogs and root beers onto the car window,

Axle continued to flirt with her. Suddenly another car caught his attention.

"Hey guys, look at who just pulled in."

The Thunderbird parked three spaces from Scams's Bonneville. The driver noticed Scams. He gave Scams a look of contempt and then stuck up his middle finger at him, flipping him the bird. That was all that Scams needed to see. He got out of the car and walked over to the Thunderbird.

"Oh shit," Axle said. "Scams, man, come back here."

Scams kept walking toward the Thunderbird. His temper was at the boiling point. When little Nicky Scambini was in a bad mood, the person he was directing his anger at was going to be in real trouble.

Most everyone was taller than Scams, but what Scams lacked in size, he made up for in strength and bravado. He did not care how big you were, or how tough you thought you were; Scams knew he was tougher. And, he usually proved to be. He walked up to the driver's side of the Thunderbird. He wasn't in a hurry; instead, he was confident and casual as he walked toward the car.

The driver of the Thunderbird and the two girls who were passengers saw Scams coming toward them. A look of concern was on their faces.

"You got a problem, asshole?" Scams asked.

"Yea, I gotta problem. The problem's you."

That was all little Nicky Scambini needed to hear. With one crushing blow, he sent a powerful punch through the open window, knocking the driver sideways into the girl sitting next to him.

Blood immediately flowed from the driver's nose, but Scams was not through. While the two girls in the car were screaming hysterically, Scams reached into the Thunderbird and began to drag the bleeding driver from the car.

"We gotta stop him, Stretch," Axle yelled as he began to get out of the Bonneville.

We both rushed over to the Thunderbird. By that time, Scams had the driver out of the car and on the ground. He was beating the defenseless driver with punch after punch. Many of the patrons had gotten out of their cars and gone over to the Thunderbird to get a better look, but no one was foolish enough to stop Scams. After a few moments, Axle and I finally pulled Scams from the badly beaten driver of the Thunderbird.

The A&W manager came out of the restaurant and told us that he had called the police. He told us to stay there until they came. If we left, he said, he would turn in Scams's license plate number. The manager took the Thunderbird driver to the restroom to be cleaned up. The driver never said a word to Scams or anyone. The two girl passengers followed the driver into the restaurant; they were crying and yelling at Scams. They called him a jerk and an asshole.

When the police arrived they took reports on what had happened. They questioned everyone involved and asked the Thunderbird driver if he wanted to press charges against Nicky Scambini. For some reason, the driver refused to do so. The two girls argued with him and told him he was crazy not to. Within half an hour of the police having arrived, the A&W was restored back to its calm atmosphere. On the way home, Scams laughed about the beating he'd given the Thunderbird driver.

When Scams's father heard about the incident, he told Scams that the only place he could drive his car to was work. For the rest of the summer, the car could not be driven for any other reason. Scams had a part-time job working at the local candle factory loading and unloading the boxcars that arrived every day. The freight train contained hundreds of boxes of wax that were used to make the candles. The job of unloading the heavy boxes of wax was tiring, and Scams hated it, but he needed the job in order to keep his car.

Axle and I also had part-time jobs. Axle worked at a local A&P supermarket bagging groceries for customers; he would also have to carry the grocery to the cars. I had the same job, but at a different store. I worked at a smaller mom and pop grocery store, just a few blocks from my home. My duties involved stocking the shelves with food items and bagging groceries. I also had to help the shoppers carry their groceries to their cars. I didn't mind that part of the job though. If I acted polite, the customers would tip me.

In the summer months, I worked during the days and on Saturdays. During the school year, I worked three days a week after school. I had been saving my money to buy a car as soon as I passed my driver's test. I'd planned on taking the test in the fall of my senior year; it was just a few months away. I had been practicing my driving with my father in his 1956 Chevy. He was very strict when it came to my driving. Any mistake I made would send him into a tyrannical outrage. His outbursts almost caused me, on a few occasions, to have accidents, but in spite of my father's screaming, I became a very good driver.

Axle and I passed the rest of that summer hanging out with Shooter. The three of us would cruise the streets of Syracuse in Shooters' '58 Chevy. Occasionally, Scams came along for the ride. He tried to talk his father into allowing him to use his car for more than just driving to work, but his father never gave in.

In October of 1964, Axle and I both passed our drivers tests. We were very excited. Axle had visions of dating every girl he could, but he still needed to work on his approach. My excitement was due to the fact that I had saved enough money for a car, and I knew what kind it was going to be. For a few months, I had my eye on a very nice '55 Chevy, two-door hardtop. It was blue with white trim and was as clean as the day it had been assembled. A friend of the family was working as a mechanic at a local Chevy dealership. Knowing that I was looking for a car, he'd mentioned the '55 Chevy to me. But, because I was not driving yet, he'd asked the dealership manager if he would hold the car for me with a down payment. The manager agreed and I picked up my car a week after I received my driver's license. I think Axle was more excited about my car than I was. He was with me when I went to the dealership on that Saturday to pick it up.

"Oh man, Stretch. This is a girl grabber," he said, as he looked the car over.

"Let's do some cruisin'."

"Ax, I have to go to work. I told you that."

"Screw work. They won't miss you."

"Can't chance it. I need the gas money now."

Axle continued to walk around the '55 Chevy, all the while expressing his admiration. After paying the remainder of my balance to the sales manager, Axle and I drove away in my Chevy for the first time.

"Hey, let's go get No Panty Annie," Axle said as he pushed the buttons of the radio looking for the right station.

"No way, Axle. I don't want that beast in my car."

"Come on man. I'll buy the Ma's Cola and the gas."

"Ax, leave the radio alone. And turn it down." He continued to pound away on the radio buttons searching for the right song.

We drove around the North Side for half an hour. I beeped the horn of my '55 Chevy at everyone we knew. Axle and I felt like royalty while friends and neighbors waved back to us.

That evening after work, I picked up Axle at his home. We cruised the streets of Syracuse and stopped at the A&W drive-in to show off my car. We'd sat there for almost an hour when Manny the Crout and his brother No-Nose pulled into the parking lot. Axle and I spotted them right away.

"Maybe the assholes won't see us," Axle remarked as he combed his hair.

"I think they already have."

Sure enough, after parking his beat-up Oldsmobile, Manny and his brother walked over to where we were parked.

"Hey, look who's here?" Manny said as he came up to me on the driver's side.

"Yea. If it ain't the Bobsie Twins," No-Nose said to his brother.

"You guys lookin' for some leg?" Manny said laughing.

"Get lost, you tards," Axle yelled.

"Hey jerk-off, whatsa matter? No nookie?" Manny screamed back.

Axle had had enough of the brothers. He started to get out of the car.

"Ax, they're not worth it. Save your strength."

"He's always in a bad mood ain't he, Stretch?" No-Nose asked.

"Why don't you guys beat it?" I told them.

"Hey, you wanna race that beast of yours?" Manny asked. He was leaning into my open window.

"Let's do it," Axle said to me. "Kick their asses. Come on?"

"Where's your balls, Stretch?" Manny asked. No-Nose stood next to Manny like a puppet, mimicking his older brother's words.

"Ha! Where's your balls? I like that Manny," No-Nose said laughing.

"Not tonight, boys," I told them. "We were leaving anyway."

Axle was upset that I did not take up Manny's challenge. But, I knew I could not afford a speeding ticket. My father would pin back my ears and take away my car if I got one.

"See you guys later," I said to Manny and No-Nose and pulled out of the A&W parking lot. A block away, Manny pulled up behind me and began tailgating.

"Guess who's behind us?" I said to Axle. "And he's right on my bumper."

Axle turned around and flipped the bird to Manny. It was dark, so we were not sure if the two brothers had noticed Axle's finger. In any event, Manny had pulled his beat-up Oldsmobile just a few inches from the bumper of my Chevy. Manny stayed close for almost three blocks. He loved to irritate people. Each time I stopped at a stop sign or a light, Manny would inch closer to my rear bumper. I could see in my rearview mirror that he and No-Nose were having the time of their life as they played their little game of cat and mouse.

"When you stop at the next intersection, I'm gonna jump out and beat his ass," Axle said as he turned around to watch the brothers.

"I am going to stop, Ax. But we'll get out just to scare them. They'll probably speed off anyway."

At that instant, Manny drove into the back of my Chevy. Not too hard, but hard enough to make me mad. I stopped the car and jumped out. Axle was out of the car before it had stopped. Manny had already backed up into a driveway and turned around. He sped off down the dark street.

"That son-of-a-bitch," I said as I pulled a flashlight from my glove box. I inspected the rear bumper for any damage; there was none that I could see.

"I told you we shoulda kicked their asses when we had the chance," Axle complained.

"We'll get 'em," I answered.

But, it was getting late, so we drove home. I inspected my car again, hoping that there was no damage. My father came out to the driveway and asked what I was doing. I told him what had happened, and he asked me if I'd broken their arms. When I told him that I hadn't, he walked away shaking his head. He went inside and slammed the door behind him.

Fifteen

I was a senior at Henninger High School, and it was no different from any other school year. My grades were average, and I skipped school quite a bit, usually with Axle. We both hated school. Axle and I held the record for the most days of missed school. Of course, Axle thought he was the record holder, but he was not even close. When our final report cards came out showing the total days missed, it was the proof I needed. We were standing in the hallway between our homerooms; Axle's class was right next to mine.

"Hey Ax, how'd you do?" I was showing him my report card. "How many days you miss?"

"Eighty-nine," he answered with a smile. "How bout you?"

"Ninety-one days," I answered as I held up my report card. "Looks like I won that bet, Ax."

"What about your grades. Do you graduate?" I asked him.

"Wow! Can you believe it? I passed everything," Axle said laughing. "Holy shit, Stretch. I'm gonna graduate. My old man is not gonna believe this. What about you?"

"Not too good, Ax. I'm short by half a credit. Can you believe it?"

"You'll graduate. Don't worry. They ain't gonna screw you for half a credit."

"They already have screwed me. I just came back from Mr. Gilbert's office and he told me that I was the one to blame and that he could not help me."

"That asshole," Axle replied. "He should be hung out the window too."

"It was gym and that damn swimming class we had to take, Ax. I flunked swimming. And that's where the half credit is missing."

Axle took the comb from his back pocket and ran it through his hair.

"Swimming? How could you flunk swimming?"

"I never went to swimming class, Ax. You know that. I can't swim. You knew that too."

Axle put his comb back in his rear pocket.

"Geez Stretch, I thought you'd learned. Even Buggers has passed swimming."

"Ax, I told Mr. Gilbert I'd tried to learn to swim. I told him that my family was all sinkers, that we aren't able to float. He thought I was being funny so he told me to leave his office."

"Whadaya gonna tell your mother and father?"

"I'll tell them I'm graduating. I'll tell them I don't wanna go to commencement. They know I hate school anyway. They'll believe me."

We walked away from the school for the last time, stopping occasionally to say goodbye to some of the students and sign yearbooks.

"See you guys at commencement," most of them said.

"Yea. See ya round," Axle replied. I said nothing.

That summer I worked every day at the grocery store. I began to hate the job, but it gave me spending money and I needed money to put gas in my car. When I was not working, I was with Axle. We played baseball and touch football, went fishing, or just hung out. Many of the Northsiders were also working, so our baseball and football games had fewer people.

Evenings in the summer of '65 were spent cruising the streets and going to dances. Neither Axle or I had a steady girlfriend, so we spent lots of time trying to find one. Axle had finally received his driver's license after failing the road test three times, but he was unable to save any money for a car. He spent every cent he earned on fishing gear, clothes, or useless items like old boat motors and broken-down car engines. Axle had parts from three old car engines lying all around his father's garage. And, like the boat motors, he had no car to put the engine in.

During our senior year though, Axle and I had managed to have girlfriends for a few weeks. The girl Axle was dating was a pretty blonde whose name was Linda Ann Fredericks. Linda Ann was a cheerleader at another high school in Syracuse.

Axle was lucky to date Linda Ann. He'd met her by accident at a dance that was being held at St. Johns High School on the Northside. Axle was standing outside the school combing his hair and smoking a Marlboro when Linda Ann had walked outdoors to get some fresh air. The pretty blonde had bumped into Axle and his cigarette slightly brushed against her arm. Axle apologized and began talking to her. He told Linda Ann that he was graduating with honors and was going to college on a baseball scholarship. He told her he'd been approached by the New York Yankees, and they wanted to sign him to a contract, but he'd told them that he would like to get his college degree first. Linda Ann could have had any boy she wanted that evening, but she chose Axle instead.

I began to date a girl who was also from another school. Her name was Beverly Lombardo. I met her at a dance at Assumption High, another Northside school. I was standing with Shooter, who was dating a girl from Assumption, at the school dance and he asked me if I wanted to meet his girl's sister. Shooter's date, Connie Lombardo, was an ugly brunette, but Shooter said he dated her for one reason only, she was a nymphomaniac. He said that Connie's sister Beverly was also one. So, Shooter introduced me to

Beverly. Beverly was much better looking than her sister, but her breath always smelled like garlic. But, because she was a nympho, I overlooked the garlic breath.

I had a '55 Chevy then and I could go parking at Schiller Park or at Crap Lake. Parking at Crap Lake was appropriately termed watching the "submarine races." I did not waste anytime in getting Beverly into the back seat of my Chevy. Every night for two weeks, with Beverly at my side, I would maneuver my Chevy back and forth between Schiller Park and Crap Lake. Beverly was a great kisser and a better tease. For two weeks, my lips became a constant fixture on Beverly's face. And, we learned every inch of the backseat of my Chevy. Hour after hour, I romanced, flirted, and begged Beverly to anoint me into manhood. I told her it was not healthy for young teenaged boys to go without sex. I mentioned to Beverly that diseases like tuberculosis and heart disease were being studied by scientists, and they were discovering that the lack of sex in young teenaged boys led to these terrible illnesses later on in life. I told her that the lack of sex in young men also caused mental illness, and she would be contributing both to science and to my health if she'd allow me to enter the temple of joy.

It never happened. After a few weeks of lip locking with Beverly Lombardo, I had to break off our courtship. I had become a walking testosterone cycle. I could take no more of her teasing, panting, and ear licking. My manhood was defeated, and I became depressed and frustrated. Just like I'd told Beverly I would. I felt beaten and my self-esteem was at an all-time low. If I can't make it with a nymphomaniac, I wondered, what will my future love life be like? I decided not to see Beverly again. I told her that seeing her was not good for my health.

Axle was having no luck with Linda Ann either. After Linda Ann discovered that Axle was not going to college on a baseball scholarship, and that the Yankees had never approached him, she dumped him for a football player at another school. But, Axle never gave up on Linda Ann. The day she broke up with him, he told her he was joining the Army and going to Vietnam. He told her that he might be killed, or come home from war maimed for life. He asked Linda Ann if it would be okay if she would have sex with him, so that he could experience what it would be like before he died. He told her that if he was going to have sex just once in his life, that he wanted it to be with her, the girl he loved. Linda Ann never gave in to Axle's request.

Although Axle and I went to the dances, we never danced. We just stood around like a pair of bookends. It was fun just standing in a corner watching the girls shake their bodies. Axle talked to many of them, but he would end up saying something stupid and the relationship would end on the same night.

Popular dance halls named Huit's, Bayhouth's and the Fayetteville Inn were crowded every evening and especially on weekends. Teenagers from all over the Syracuse area would gather to listen to bands named Sam and The Twisters, or The Mystics. And, if you were eighteen years old, you could drink alcohol legally.

Neither Axle nor I were eighteen, so we sipped Coca-Cola or Pepsi and waited patiently until we reached the age of another rite of passage. Some of the Northsiders like Scams and Shooter and Manny the Crout were already eighteen and drinking. Scams and Shooter could not hold their liquor well and usually got into fights. There was one night in particular when there were two incidents involving Scams, Shooter and Manny. Each happened at almost the same exact time.

Bayhouth's was crowded on that Friday night. Scams had been drinking beer and decided to walk outside for some fresh air. Shooter was mixing his drinks, drinking everything he could. He began dancing with a lovely dark-haired girl.

Shooter was drunk and having a great time. Axle had finally coerced a short, buxom brunette to get into my parked Chevy with him. The car was parked behind the dance hall in the parking lot. I was inside talking with Scurvy Sam Giambollo and Baby Face Cosmo Cosantine, Shooter's brother. Scurvy had hitched a ride that evening with Axle and me, and Baby Face had come to the dance with Shooter. Axle later told me what had happened outside. I witnessed what was about to happen inside Bayhouth's.

When Axle was in my car making out with the brunette, he suddenly heard a loud scream. He told me it sounded like Tarzan. Axle and the girl became frightened and immediately looked out the car window. They saw Scams running with his head down, like he was about to make a diving tackle. His target was Manny the Crout. Manny was standing in front of Scams' car. He was pissing on the hood. No-Nose and Manny were laughing as the warm pee splashed from the hood of the Pontiac.

Scams had just walked around the back corner of the parking lot when he witnessed what was happening. His dive into Manny was brutal. While screaming like Tarzan, he knocked Manny hard into the dance club wall. Manny fell to the ground and covered his face. The Crout never had a chance to zip up and put his penis back. Scams beat and kicked him mercilessly. No-Nose ran into the club to call for help.

In the meantime, events inside the dance hall had taken a similar turn. The girl Shooter was dancing with had come with a date. Her date, a big brute of a football player, noticed Shooter dancing with her. He had just returned from the bar and walked up to Shooter and the girl on the dance floor. He was carrying a bottle of beer with him.

"This is my girl, asshole."

"Hey numb-nuts, I'm just dancin' with her. Back off."

"What did you call me?" Brutus asked.

The girl and Shooter stopped dancing. The pretty brunette told her boyfriend it was just a harmless dance.

I saw what happened next and was amazed that Shooter was not killed. After the girl's remark, Brutus smashed his beer bottle over Shooter's head. The brunette began screaming and crying and she called Brutus names like jerk, asshole, and creep.

Meanwhile, Shooter lay on the floor bleeding from a large cut on the side of his head. As he lay there moaning and writhing with pain, the bouncer came over and told the guy that the police were on their way and that he was to stay where he was. Of course, Brutus wanted no part of that. As he began to leave, the bouncer grabbed him and the two began throwing punches and wrestling with each other. While this was happening inside the club, Axle came running in with No-Nose, who'd left the scene outside. He told me that Scams was beating the hell out of Manny for pissing on his car.

My concern, though, was for Shooter. He was still lying on the floor. He was conscious and bleeding from his head but he was okay. The fight between the bouncer and the boyfriend ended with the bouncer putting a headlock on the football player as the cops arrived.

Shooter was taken to the emergency room with a slight concussion. His parents stayed at the hospital all night and pressed charges against the football player. Shooter recovered within a few days. After that incident, Shooter used to say to us that if his head wasn't as hard as it was, he would probably be a vegetable. We all agreed.

During that summer, I thought quite a bit about what I would do with my life. I was working at a grocery store and had no high school diploma. I wondered about where I was headed. I did not have the motivation to look elsewhere for work, or even a career. I just hung out with Axle.

Axle had been talking about going into the Army. He thought that if he learned a trade in the service he could get a good paying job when he came out. Of course, Axle always talked about doing things and then never followed through on them. The idea of going into the service never entered my mind. Even though I was of draft age, as were most of my North Side friends, I did not want to enlist, with the possibility of ending up in Vietnam and fighting in a war I knew very little about. My father, the ex-marine, thought that going into the service was a good idea. He also thought that I would be able to learn a trade and when discharged have the opportunity to find a good job.

My father never told me to stay out of the service. He never told me to stay away from war either. Nor did my mother ever say anything about whether I should enlist. I think she thought that whatever road I choose for my life would be okay with her.

In the summer of '65, the Vietnam war was becoming more and more of a news event. Every evening on the local station, reporters were talking with American GIs who were in Vietnam. The reporters would ask questions like, "How do you feel about being over here?" or "What's it like to see your friends being killed?" "Do you believe in what you're doing?" The young GIs tried to answer their questions as diplomatically as they could. They tried to be honest, but you could sense that what they were saying was not what they were really feeling. Sometimes though, their real emotions would show, and they would be crying.

Each day the newspapers showed front-page news about the war. Many times, bold headlines announced atrocities of the war. By the end of that summer of '65, there were a few Northsiders enlisting in various branches of the service. Shooter and Jimmy the Skidmarks enlisted in the Air Force; Scams joined the Army. Others, like me, just waited to see what would happen. I thought about the possibility of being drafted into the Army, but I was hoping that the war in

Vietnam would go away and my problem would be solved. I still thought about Heinzie and what had happened to him. I was confused, scared and alone with my problem. I began to pray more. Alone, in my room, I would ask God to help me figure out how I would deal with the draft, the war and my life's work. I did not want to end up like Heinze.

When we were younger, we would play war. We all had toy guns, plastic helmets and canteens. We would shoot each other and make believe we were dead. Some of us became heroes. I would force my younger brother Richard to be the enemy. Sometimes he was a Jap, sometimes a German, but always the enemy. I would be Audi Murphy or Sgt. York. I made my brother hide in the neighborhood and told him to surprise me with an attack. Then, off I would go with my toy rifle in the ready position prepared for an ambush. But, my brother was not a smart enemy; he used to hide in the same places. It was easy for me to sneak up on him, surprise him, and then shoot him dead. Just like Audi Murphy and Sgt. York in the movies.

Axle was a good enemy. I could never find him. He would search the neighborhood looking for the best places to hide. Sometimes he hid behind North High School, in the bushes. Other times he would hide in the alley between the houses on Lilac Street. The neighbors would come out of their homes and yell at him. Axle would just point his gun and shoot them.

When patrolling the neighborhood, I could never find Axle in time. He would always jump from his hiding place, screaming like a banshee, and kill Audi Murphy, or Sgt. York. Then he would take his canteen from his belt and have a drink of water. Sometimes, Axle would just capture me. He would march me down the street, his toy gun pointed at my back as he led me to the enemy's camp. Either way, Axle won the war.

Playing war games as kids was just that, a game. The loser, who was killed during the game, was able to wake up from his death and play another battle. Sometimes we would die three or four times in one day. There was a lot of death from war battles on the North Side during the '50s and the '60s. And as many times as we were killed, we always healed ourselves, reloaded our plastic guns and went off to fight yet another battle. And at the end of the day, we would fall asleep and dream about tomorrow's battle.

Sixteen

My first job was as a paperboy. I was eleven years old. I delivered the evening newspapers around the neighborhood. Each afternoon, I picked up my papers at an old, musty building where a street hustler named Shifty operated his distributorship. Shifty was my first boss. No one knew Shifty's real name. At least that was what all the kids had said. At the time I took the job, I didn't know that Shifty was a thief. I soon found out that his nickname fit him perfectly.

I walked into his musty little business one morning and asked if I could deliver papers. He was a mean man with a hot temper. He did not like kids either; he treated all of his paperboys with an unfriendly demeanor and harsh words. I knew from the start that Shifty was not one to mess with, but I needed the job. Shifty hired me that day and told me what he expected from me.

"You try and cheat me kid," he was talking through a cloud of cigar smoke, "and your ass is mine. You understand?" The cigar dangled from his lips. The end was wet and chewed away.

Shifty gave me a route that was about three blocks from my home. He told me to pick up my papers at 3 p.m. every afternoon and get them delivered by 5 p.m., or else. He told me he wanted me at his musty building at 5 a.m. on Sunday mornings to deliver the Sunday morning paper by 7 a.m., or else.

When it came time for me to collect my money from the customers on Fridays, Shifty told me I'd better get all the money collected and turned into him no later than Saturday at 3 p.m., or else. He told me that if I was short with the amount of money I collected each week, and what was owed to him, that he would use my tip money to make up the difference, or else. I was afraid of Shifty and tried very hard to please him.

My paper route consisted of seventy-two customers. Each day after school, I would hurry home, get my wagon, and proceed to the musty building to pick up my papers. Shifty never greeted any of his paperboys with a hello. Instead, he would say, "Get your papers counted and get outta here." It usually took me an hour and a half to deliver all of my papers. On Sunday mornings, it would take me less time to deliver the papers. That was because the old apartment buildings on my route scared me. There were some strange people living in those buildings. Often, I would hear families yelling and screaming, and many times the police were there to calm things down. So, on Sunday mornings, even though everyone was sleeping, I would race through the buildings as fast as I could.

I hated getting up at 4:30 every Sunday morning, and I hated the idea of delivering papers in those old apartment buildings at that time of the day. Besides the strange people who lived there, the buildings were dark and eerie. I would run up the five flights of stairs as quickly as I could and drop the newspapers in front of the apartments on each floor. Then, I would quickly run back down the stairs and out the door. The dark, haunting, and spooky buildings gave me the creeps. I hated Shifty even more for having me deliver to those buildings.

Each week, when it came time for me to collect from my customers, I always had a problem. Many of them would not pay me. They always had excuses why they did not have any money for me that week. Others, but not many, paid on time, and a few always tipped me. That was how we made our money each week. We depended on our tips.

Our tips were important because we did not receive an hourly wage for delivering the newspapers. Many times, weeks would go by and certain customers, mostly the weird ones who lived in the apartment buildings, would run up bills. And because the paperboys were responsible for paying for the newspapers, if we did not collect enough to pay for them, Shifty would keep our tips as payment, just like he'd promised.

There were many weeks when I delivered newspapers with no payments from my customers, so Shifty would keep my tips. I tried very hard to collect from the slow payers, but they would never come up with the money. Shifty would take my tips saying, "You'll learn the hard way kid, or not at all," always puffing on a cigar with the ends chewed off. After a while, I had to stop delivery to the nonpayers, but I still tried to collect from them what they'd owed me. I never told my mother or father that I had been working for nothing. I knew that if my father found out about what Shifty had been doing with my tips, I would have to pay the consequences, and so would the cigar chewing Shifty. Unfortunately, my father did find out one evening. He heard from Axle's dad that I was not being paid.

When he confronted me, I reluctantly told him the truth. I told my father how Shifty treated me and how he kept my tip money. My father screamed at me for being taken advantage of. He told me to stand up for myself and to go after what was mine, or else I would always be at the mercy of others.

The next day, after work, my father went with me to pick up my newspapers. Shifty was standing behind the dirty counter. The counter was full of newspapers that were going to be delivered that day. Shifty was puffing on a cigar and yelling at his paperboys. When my father and I walked into the building, Shifty looked up at the two of us; he was startled to see my father with me. My father wasted no time.

"You the boss?" my father asked.

Shifty puffed frantically on his chewed-up cigar. He talked through the smoke that swirled around his head.

"That's me. Hey kid, here's your papers," he said, never looking up at my father.

"He's not delivering," my father said with authority.

Shifty looked up at my father and puffed a cloud of smoke in his direction. I felt the tension between them.

"Oh, is that right? You gonna deliver them for him?" he asked sarcastically.

"No, I'm not gonna deliver them, and neither is my son. We're here to collect the money you owe him."

Shifty was still puffing frantically on his cigar; he continued to scream at one of the paperboys.

"I don't owe him nothin'," he said without looking up.

In an instant, I realized for the first time just how tough my father could be. I knew at that moment, when my father reached over the counter, grabbed Shifty by his shirt, yanked him toward him, and smacked him hard on his nose that my father was acting the only way he knew how to. He'd grown up in a time when being tough meant surviving. The North Side I was growing up in was, according to my father, softer than it had been in the past. Although the North Side was changing at the time my father punched out Shifty, it was not until many years later that I realized it had begun a metamorphosis years before.

I realized that the North Side had always been changing, and that it always would be. It had to change. Nothing ever stays the same. People change, animals evolve. Cars become faster and sleeker. Erosion wastes away shorelines and changes their contours. Cities grow and prosper, or they disintegrate. Old diseases are beaten with new drugs, and new diseases take over. The North Side had been disintegrating for years. And, as much as I wanted to believe that the North Side would once again stand proud, I knew that would never happen. It was beyond repair. There were too many Shiftys living there, and not enough tough ex-marines to claim the North Side back.

Sure, street toughs like my father still roam the North Side. However, unlike my father, the new thugs carry guns and knives and do not care who they hurt. The punks of today who threaten the Northsiders have no respect for anyone, not even their families. My father's gang of bad boys was just that, bad boys, but they had respect for their families. The street punks who roam the North Side today will kill their parents and siblings for drugs or a dollar. My father would only hurt you if you treated him with disrespect, or if you took from him what was not yours. The only time he would mug someone was during a game of poker down at Rocco's Bar and Grill. Cheating by dealing from the bottom of the deck was not going to upset the social structure of the North Side. The cheating made some people angry, but the next day they would be back to playing poker again.

The real change to the North Side came when my family and my father's family moved away. It continued when the families of Axle, Shooter, Scurvy Sam and the rest of our gang moved away. The history of the North Side evolved into another chapter when those families who had respect for others moved away, and a new family of young thugs moved in and replaced them. On that day when my father smacked Shifty and bloodied his face for the few dollars that Shifty had owed me, my father was teaching me a lesson the best way he knew how. And that lesson was that the world was a place where either you eat, or you get eaten. My father knew that the North Side was beginning to change, that it was becoming a tougher place to live in, and he wanted me to understand how to survive its streets. If I survived there, then I could fit in anywhere.

Seventeen

Axle and I called Onondaga Lake in Syracuse, "Crap Lake." One reason was because the Lake was terribly polluted with everything from chemicals dumped by local factories to human excrement. Often times when we fished the lake or one of its tributaries, we would see toilet paper floating on top of the water. It was because of the chemicals discarded into the lake that Axle and I believed the carp in the lake were so big. We assumed that the chemicals were abnormally increasing the growth of the carp. Because human crap floated in the lake, and the words crap and carp contained the same letters, we brilliantly gave Onondaga Lake its new name of Crap Lake.

Axle and I loved to fish there because the carp were monstrous. During the summer months, before we were fortunate enough to own bicycles, we would walk the four miles to Crap Lake. We carried our fishing gear and a loaf of bread. The bread was used to make dough balls; the carp loved dough balls. Axle and I would wet a piece of bread, then roll it into a ball and place it securely on the hook. We would cast into the lake from the rocky shoreline and wait patiently for that massive strike.

The carp is an ugly fish. Axle used to say that the carp was almost as ugly as Mary "The Leopard" Mott. Mary was a girl who lived on the North Side and attended the same schools we did. We called her "The Leopard" because she had yellow and brown blotches that dotted her face. No one knew why Mary was covered with those spots. We figured she had an incurable disease, and if we accidentally touched her, or even went near her, then we would catch the dreaded disease.

Everyone made fun of Mary. We called her names and laughed at how she dressed. The Leopard was always dirty. Her clothes were filled with holes. Mary "The Leopard"

Mott was probably colorblind as well. Her clothes never matched. They were a contrast of colors. And she smelled bad too. Her body odor could be detected two classrooms away. We avoided her like the plague; even the girls on the North Side avoided the Leopard, except for one. Mary's only friend was No Panty Annie.

The two girls were always together. They were a perfect fit for one another. Both were outcasts of the North Side, and both girls were the only children in their families. They were not great students, but they did not miss much school. For all the harassment the girls took from the other students, the two outcasts always went to school. They even managed to get most of their classes together. Axle and I wondered how they managed to do that. All through junior and senior high school, Axle and I had tried to get the same classes, but the school officials always split us up. A few times both girls were in our classes. When that happened, Axle and I skipped school more often. Our excuse was that we were afraid of catching Mary The Leopard's dreaded disease.

After a morning of fishing, if Axle and I were lucky enough to catch any carp, we would take them down to the south side of Syracuse and sell them to the African Americans. It was easier to sell them when we had our bikes. The walk to the south side from Crap Lake took about two hours. But, if the fish were large, we knew we could make a killing selling them. The African Americans loved them.

When we had our bikes, we would wrap the carp in newspapers and set them in our front baskets. The ride to the south side would take about an hour. When we arrived there, Axle and I would pull up to any African American we saw and tell them what we had. If they were interested, we would show them the carp. Usually there was some price haggling that went on; after a while, Axle and I became great negotiators for our young ages.

The price would normally start at around $.25 each for a small carp and up to $2.00 for the large ones. We never went home without selling all of our fish. But, usually by the time Axle and I returned home, we were out of money. Because we had not eaten all day, we would stop at the first grocery store we saw and buy cokes, potato chips, Hostess Twinkies and Cracker Jacks. By the time we reached our homes it would be late in the day. Our parents would scream at us for being gone all day and then try to force us to eat dinner, especially my mother. They didn't know that we had just gorged ourselves on junk food.

"You're hungry," my mother would say, always assuming that I was hungry. And the conversation was always the same.

"No, I'm not, Mom."

"And you smell like fish. Go wash before you eat."

My mother was always leaning over the stove cooking something. Pasta, sauce, peppers and eggs; the aroma of food constantly filled the house on the North Side.

"Here, sit down and eat some homemade macaroni," she would say while setting a plate filled with food in front of me.

"Mom, I'm not hungry."

"Yes, you are. You've been gone all day."

"No really. I'm not hungry."

"You want some milk?"

"I don't want anything. I'm not hungry."

"Here. Have two meatballs."

"I don't want any meatballs." Then she would drop two large meatballs into my plate of macaroni.

"Your brother ate four meatballs at dinner time."

"That's nice, Mom. But I'm not hungry."

If my father was home, he would walk into the kitchen and stare at me, and not say a word. I would force down the food and then walk away from the table burping up sauce because my stomach would be so full. My mother would congratulate me on finishing my dinner.

Fishing was just one of the outdoor activities that Axle and I enjoyed doing together during the summer months. Another past time that we had was shooting rats with our .22 rifles. Rats as large as cats roamed the area in front of Crap Lake. It was a wooded area and thick with hardwoods and years of garbage dumping. The rats loved the garbage, and Axle and I loved killing the rats.

Shooting our rifles in the middle of the city was against the law. But, when it came to hunting rats, Axle and I figured we were doing the city and our neighbors a service by killing the rats. Usually, we started in the morning, after our parents had left for work. We didn't want them to see us leaving our homes with our rifles. Then Axle and I would stroll confidently down the streets of Syracuse carrying our guns like a pair of big-game hunters. Had our parents known what we were up to, they would have grounded us for the rest of the summer.

Axle was a great shot. He could shoot a rat while the rat was on a dead run. I usually missed. I injured more rats than I killed. Axle used to say that I shot my gun like a girl.

"Stretch," he would say, "you gotta squeeeeeze the trigger easy. And breathe out while you squeeeeeze the trigger."

The rats I killed had to be shot two or three times before they died. Axle killed his rats with one, well-placed bullet. Axle's rats dropped instantly. My rats ran around in circles, dazed and confused after I'd shot them. I had to walk up to them and shoot them again until they stopped flopping around on the ground.

We always went home after our safari before our parents came home from work. When they asked us what we had done during the day, we would tell them we had gone fishing or played baseball. Lying to our parents at that age was the common thing to do. If we hadn't lied to them, Axle and I would not have been able to do some of the things we enjoyed doing. Hunting in the city limits, riding boxcars, drinking wine in the church rectory and skipping school were not activities that our parents would have allowed us to do; our only choice was to lie. I also forced my brother and sisters to lie on my behalf. If they failed to lie for me, then they would suffer the consequences.

My younger brother Rich almost paid dearly for not lying for me one day. I had walked into my home with my .22 slung over my shoulder, and my mother was home. She had come home from work early that day because she was not feeling well. When she'd asked my brother where I was, Rich had told her I was with Axle and that we had our guns with us.

My mother screamed at my brother, "Madre della Madonna. Dove? Dove?" (Holy mother of God. Where? Where?) My seven-year-old brother had begun to cry.

"I don't know where he went, Mama."

My brother had seen me leave with my rifle that morning. My sisters were still sleeping. I'd told my brother that if ever Mom or Dad came home before I did, to tell them that I was taking my rifle to the gun shop to get a price for selling it. That would give me the excuse for taking the rifle from my home. I told my brother that if he did not tell that story, and I got into trouble, I would beat him up and hide his body where no one would ever find it. Instead of lying for me, Rich told the truth.

When I came home and walked down the driveway to my backdoor, I could smell sauce cooking. I hoped the smell was not coming from our kitchen. As I walked into the kitchen with my rifle over my shoulder, my mother was waiting for me. She wiped her hands on her apron and told me to not say a word and to sit down. I could tell by the expression on her face and the tone of her voice that I was in big trouble and it was best that I do what she asked. I sat down at the kitchen table and laid my .22 on the floor.

My mother walked around the kitchen trying to find something to hit me with. She opened all of the drawers.

"Where's my wooden spoon?"

"Mom?"

She kept slamming the drawers open and closed, looking for that spoon.

"You shut your mouth," she said as she turned toward me.

I was already thinking about how I was going to torture my brother. I knew he'd told my mother where I was without her even asking him. My brother was standing behind the ironing board crying. He was mumbling to my mother about how I was going to beat him up, kill him and then hide his body where no one would ever find him.

"No he's not," my mother said to Rich.

"If anyone is going to be dead from a beating, it will be HIM." My mother now focused her attention on the kitchen cabinets.

"Where's that spoon?" She slammed the doors of the cabinets closed.

"Mom? Will you let me explain?" I asked. But, I didn't have an explanation. I just thought that it was the right thing to say until I thought of something else.

"Wait till your father gets home." She stopped looking for her weapon and turned toward me.

"But Mom?"

"Don't you 'but mom' me, young man." She shook her finger at me. For a brief moment, I thought I was gaining an edge. She sat down. Mom was tired from pacing the floor and looking for the wooden spoon.

"You were shooting that gun in the city weren't you?"

"Yes but . . ."

"You shut up. You just wait till your father hears about this."

"Yes but . . ."

"Shut your mouth. Don't you know you're breaking the law? We've talked about this before."

"Yes mom, but let me . . ."

"I told you to keep quiet."

My father never did find out about that incident with the rifle. My mother had calmed down by the time he came home from work. But, she did take away some of my privileges. I could not fish for the rest of the summer, nor could I ever shoot my .22 rifle anywhere without an adult being with me. She made me promise her I would never take my gun into the city again. The promise lasted one week. The following week Axle and I were hunting rats at the city dump. And, from that time on, I hid my rifle under the front porch of my home, where it would be easy for me to retrieve it and put it back whenever I wanted to hunt with Axle. I was never caught again.

Axle's mom and dad were more lenient with Axle. I was always jealous of that. It seemed as if Axle could do anything, or go anywhere, without his parents questioning him. I think that was the reason Axle did things without thinking them through. He knew he had no one to answer to if things went bad.

Axle's dad was never home. He was a traveling salesman and always away from home. Axle's mom worked as a receptionist at a doctor's office. She was never home because she belonged to different clubs and organizations. That left Axle with plenty of time away from his parents in which to do stupid things, and not get caught doing them. Axle's dad had a bad temper along with a drinking problem. The two were a bad mixture. I remember a few times when Axle had been beaten by his father. Sometimes we could hear the beatings taking place, but no one ever interfered. Axle's dad scared me more than any adult I knew.

Sometimes, Axle and I would break the windows at the old North High School. We would throw stones at them to see who could break the most. One day Axle was caught by a policeman. A neighbor had heard the windows breaking and called the police department. When Axle's dad found out, he beat Axle with a belt. He beat Axle so badly that Axle had welts on his back for two weeks. Axle hated his father and he seemed to just accept his mother. Axle's mom never showed any love toward him. It was the same way between Axle's mother and father. Many times Axle had mentioned to me that his parents were going to get a divorce. They fought constantly. As Axle grew older, the arguments intensified. Axle used to tell me that he'd always thought that he was the reason for his parents' unhappiness. He had wished many times that they would divorce and that his father would move away. That way he could live more peacefully and without the tension that always surrounded his home. Many times, I felt sorry for Axle. I wished I could have adopted him as my brother and he could live with me. And Axle cared the same way about me. That was why we did the next best thing to adopting each other. We became blood brothers.

We were ten years old when we decided to become brothers. The ceremony was to take place at Skeleton Island. We had everything we needed packed away in our pockets. There were the usual items, some spuds, a saltshaker, matches, and canteens of water, hanging from our belts. We also carried Band-Aids and two brand new pocketknives. We figured a special occasion like this needed special knives. Both knives were identical. We'd purchased them at Sears and Roebuck. They were red Swiss Army knives, expensive, but beautiful in design, perfect for the occasion. We'd had the knives specially engraved. Axle and I had the engraving done by a friend of my mother's who was a jeweler. When I told him who my mother was, he said he would give us his best engraving for free. Axle and I were excited that we did not have to pay for the engraving. After purchasing the knives, we'd had no money left. The kind jeweler asked us what we had in mind for the engraving. Axle and I knew the words that we wanted to have engraved on our knives. Inscribed on my knife were the words, "For my friend Dickey Axle Palumbo." Axle's knife would read, "For my friend Frankie Stretch Pandozzi." The jeweler told us they would be fine engravings and then carved the words onto the outer case of each knife.

On the summer morning of the ceremony, it was already hot and humid when Axle and I walked toward Skeleton Island. As we walked, we talked about how the day would cement our friendship forever. From that day forward, we would always take care of each other. Nothing would interfere with our friendship. No one could harm one without doing harm to the other. If you mistreated one of us, then that would mean you would be confronted by the other, or both of us.

Our bond would also mean that if we had to, we would lie for each other. To Axle and me, lying was a part of growing up. It was a way to get what we wanted. And, if lying to protect each other worked, it was okay to do so, because then it meant that the lying did what it was suppose to do—protect each of us from the truth.

When we arrived at Skeleton Island, we crossed a small stream that emptied into the swamp. There was a small grove of oak trees shading an area covered in grass and myrtle. A willow tree stood all alone. Its huge, sweeping branches hung low, almost sweeping the ground. Our ceremony would take place beneath the shade of that willow tree.

Axle and I arrived at the decisive moment. There would be no turning back. We had planned this moment for weeks. We sat down under the shade of the drooping willow tree and took our knives from our pockets. Carefully, we opened the blades and cleaned them with water from our canteens. I heard a robin sing and saw a cottontail rabbit scurry across the ground in front of us. We were ready; there was no hesitation as Axle and I sliced our forefingers with our Swiss Army knives. The blood dripped from our cuts. As the blood oozed, Axle and I pressed our fingers together. Our blood mixed, connecting us forever.

The cottontail came back. It stopped briefly to watch us, then scampered off. Axle did his best "what's up doc?" Bugs Bunny imitation. We both laughed as we sat under the willow tree bandaging our fingers. When we'd finished our ceremony, we exchanged our Swiss Army knives, as a token of our friendship. We promised each other that our knives would never be used for any other purpose, and that we would always carry them as a token of our friendship.

As the morning moved into late afternoon, Axle and I built a fire and ate our spuds. We hiked through the island woods and climbed a cherry tree. We stayed in the tree for an hour as we picked and ate the ripe fruit. The day grew hotter and our water from our canteens was gone. It was time to head home. As Axle and I walked from the shade of Skeleton Island, I looked back toward that willow tree. The cottontail had hopped back to its spot under the tree. It wrinkled its nose a few times and watched us walk away.

Eighteen

The first time I realized I was not a very good athlete was when I tried out for the junior varsity football team at North High. Axle and Shooter talked me into it. They told me the team was so bad that no one wanted to play for them, and that coach Bartolo would take anyone who could walk straight. After listening to Axle and Shooter's pep talk, I believed I could make the team. Axle and Shooter didn't try out for the team, however. They claimed they had other commitments.

I decided to try out for the offensive end position. I was good at catching a football, and I was tall. Being tall was good if you wanted to play the end position in football. When the Northsiders got together for a touch football game, or a game of tackle, I always played the end position. And, when the ball was thrown my way, I usually caught it. However, I soon found out that football played by a bunch of friends versus football played by a high school team, where every player is bigger and faster than you are, well, that was a different story. During a football game with your friends, you can make mistakes and get away with it. And, those games are played innocently. But when you try out for a high school team things become different. Those Northsiders who previously were your friends playing a friendly game of touch football are suddenly trying to take your head off during football practice. Everyone wants to make the team. Even though past years showed no promise for the team's future, those kids wanted to be jocks, and I wanted to be a jock too. I soon found out that I was better off playing dodge ball during gym class than being a tackling dummy for the football team.

I was skinny. My height had a higher number than my weight did. I was also slow. I knew my running speed was no better than a slow turtle. So, it was no surprise to me that the first time I showed up for practice and caught the football as an offensive end, my face was immediately introduced to the ground. Arthur Kolakowski hit me with a vicious, bone-crunching tackle. Everyone called Arthur "psycho." He had a bad temper. Arthur was also big. He weighed almost three hundred pounds. So when I was tackled by "psycho," as I lay on the ground face down in the dirt, I began to wonder if playing football on a high school team was a smart thing. But I got up from the ground and tried again. However, I did become smarter. Every time the ball came my way to catch, I would drop it on purpose. It seemed like Arthur was always in my area, ready to punish me.

Coach Bartolo screamed at me a lot. "Pandozzi. Run, run, run. My grandmother runs faster." However, the faster I tried to run, the slower I became. When my brain told my legs to move faster, confusion set in. It was as if the communication between my brain and my legs had faulty wiring. Like when the telephone line is cut and you can't make a phone call. The line is there, but the message can't go through. That's the way it was when I was running. So, one day when Coach Bartolo was yelling, "Pandozzi. You have two speeds. Slow and slower," I decided that my football days were over. I figured that between Arthur trying to rearrange my body parts and Coach Bartolo's psychological encouragement, it was perhaps best for my body and soul to stick with dodge ball.

I had an advantage playing dodge ball because I was so skinny. I was usually one of the last to be standing. I used my skinniness to my advantage. When the ball came toward me, I would turn sideways and the ball would whisk right past me. I would frustrate the players on the other side because they couldn't hit me. Unless, of course, Little Nicky Scams Scambini was playing.

Scams could throw the dodge ball faster and harder than anyone on the North Side, maybe even in the whole city of Syracuse. When Scams threw the dodge ball in your direction, you only had a split second to move out of the way, or else you would end up stinging with pain from where the ball had hit you. Every time Scams threw the ball, he'd hit someone. And, when it came down to Scams and me alone, Scams usually won. I could turn sideways and have Scams' shot miss me only so often. Sooner or later, Scams would get me out.

Playing dodge ball at Franklin Elementary School was a frequent pastime. Even though we were students in junior high or high school, we spent many evenings playing dodge ball at Franklin. Shooter, Axle, Boogers, Scams, Two Toes, Manny and No-Nose, Skidmarks, and Baby Face were always there. Usually each side consisted of the same players with Scams' team winning most games.

Franklin Elementary was usually open for recreational purposes in the evenings from seven o'clock until ten o'clock. Those were the days when we could walk the streets of the North Side without worrying about being the victim of a vicious assault. Our parents never had to worry about us. The streets were free from crime and drugs. Only occasionally was there ever any lawbreaking of a felonious nature against a Northsider walking the streets at night. But, there was one evening when an incident occurred against one of our North Side friends as he walked from his home to Franklin.

Boogers Freeman Polanski walked into the gym at Franklin Elementary bloodied and beaten. We ran to his aid and questioned him about what had happened. Boogers was shaken and still scared from the assault. He'd walked four blocks from where he had been attacked. Although Boogers was not too smart and wasn't the most popular person in school, we all watched out for his well-being. That night was no different. Scams started questioning Boogers about what had happened.

"I-I-I wa-wa-was wa-walking d-d-down P-p-p-park Street." Scams told Boogers to sit down and try to talk slower. Boogers sat down and leaned back against the gymnasium wall. Snot dripped from his nose. He wiped his nose with the back of his hands.

"They ja-ja-jumped out of a ca-ca-car an' hi-hi-hit m-m-me."

"What kinda car?" Axle asked. Boogers was not too smart, but he knew his cars. He could name any car and year instantly by looking at the front and back grills.

"I-i-i-it wa-wa-was a n-nine-teen fif-fifty s-s-seven Chevy. Gr-gr-een, wi-with a wa-wa-white t-t-top. Cr-crome-reversed wa-wheels."

"Do you know who they were?" Scams asked.

"They sa-sa-said they wa-wa-were f-from the Va-Va-Valley."

"Son of a bitches!" Scams yelled out. "It's those bastard Crusaders."

Everyone in Syracuse knew who the Crusaders were. They were a gang of punks from the southwest side of the city. Occasionally, they traveled to other areas of the city and terrorized the innocent. Scams told Boogers not to worry. He told him it was payback time. Scams, Shooter and his brother Baby Face, along with Axle and Harry Armpits Hertz, piled into Scams's father's Oldsmobile and drove to the Valley looking for the Crusaders. I helped Boogers walk home. He was still scared and had trouble with his balance. We found out later that Boogers had sustained a slight concussion from the beating, but within a few days, he was back to his old self.

Scams was one of the older Northsiders and had begun driving a few months earlier. However, he was only sixteen and unable to drive at night. The legal age to drive without adult supervision was seventeen, if you had passed drivers education. Scams had passed the course but still had a few months to go before he reached the legal age. That small detail, however, did not stop him from rolling out his father's Olds from the driveway at his home that evening. Scams needed to sneak the car away while his mother and father watched their favorite evening television programs. Once Scams rolled the Oldsmobile down the driveway onto the street, he could use his spare key to start the car and drive away. But, if he were caught by his father, he would be grounded for the rest of the summer. It was not the first time that Little Nicky Scambini had snuck his parents' car from the driveway of their home. He had managed to sneak the automobile out on several occasions, and he'd never got caught. Each time he became bolder and less afraid. On the night that Boogers was beaten, Scams got in front of the car and began to push it very slowly down the driveway.

Shooter was behind the wheel, he maneuvered the Olds toward the street. Axle sat next to Shooter and Harry Armpits and Baby Face sat in the back. When Shooter had finished guiding the car into the dark street, he climbed into the back with Armpits and Baby Face. Scams got behind the wheel, started the engine and within seconds began driving toward the southwest side of the city.

"I know where those guys hang out," Armpits said.

"Yea, me too," Axle replied as he combed his hair.

"What are ya combing your hair for?" Shooter asked sarcastically. "We're going to a rumble."

The five friends joked with each other while Scams drove down South Salina Street. Behind the joking, they knew the chance they were taking by stealing Scams' parents' car. And, to add to the seriousness of the night, the group was carrying baseball bats and brass knuckles with them. The brass knuckles had been purchased illegally by Scams. A few months earlier, a North Side hood called "Bones" had told Scams that brass knuckles were good to have and you never knew when you would need them. He sold them to Scams for two dollars.

And now, a few months later, the brass knuckles might be needed. Their friend had been beaten and humiliated, and that act would not be tolerated by the Northsiders, especially the Back Alley Boys. If it took brass knuckles and bats to even the score, then that was what the Northsiders would use. Justice needed to be served. There was an unwritten law amongst the Back Alley friends. It was a silent code of honor that was worn proudly in their hearts. Scams kept repeating the unwritten law as he searched for his prey. "Mess with one of us, and you have to deal with all of us." In a few moments, all five friends were chanting the unwritten law.

Scams also knew where the Southwest kids hung out. There was a park in the valley named Roosevelt Park, and across from the park was a Bob's Big Boy drive-in restaurant. It was like the A&W restaurant on the other side of the city. The park and the drive-in restaurant were popular hangouts for the Valley crowd.

Scams pulled the Olds into the parking lot of Bob's Big Boy; it was 9:30 p.m. The parking lot was filled with teenagers and their cars. Scams didn't park; instead, he drove slowly through the parking lot looking for the '57 Chevy that Boogers had described. Almost at the same time as Scams and the Northsiders were driving through the parking lot, the green '57 Chevy with chrome-reversed wheels pulled into a parking space. Scams and the other Northsiders saw the Chevy immediately. Scams parked the Olds three spaces away.

The Chevy had six passengers. They were wild and unruly. They were screaming obscenities at innocent teenagers. Everyone tried to ignore the ruffians, that is, except for Scams and his North Side friends. They watched the group in the Chevy with anger. They talked about Boogers' bruises and how the Crusaders would pay for the pain they'd caused their friend. All the while, they waited patiently until the time was right. The Northsiders did not want to have an altercation at the drive-in restaurant. Within minutes, two of the bullies got out of the Chevy and walked up to a white Plymouth with two giggling teenage girls. Words were exchanged, and then there was screaming between the two bullies and the girls. One of the young thugs began to pound on the hood of the girls' car. Scams and the Northsiders watched as the two bullies returned to the Chevy. The driver of the car started the engine and drove from the parking lot; Scams followed close behind.

The Chevy pulled into Roosevelt Park across the street. As Scams followed in the Oldsmobile, the car with the girls also drove into the park. Scams stopped the Olds and watched the car of bullies and the car with the girls park next to each other. Once again, the two ruffians got out of the car and approached the girls. The four other occupants of the Chevy were talking loudly, hanging their heads from the Chevy's windows and screaming at no one in particular. An argument between the two bullies and the two girls in the Plymouth started again.

While the screaming between the two girls and the two ruffians grew louder, the four occupants of the Chevy noticed Scams and his friends watching them intently. All four of them got out of their car and walked toward Scams and the Olds. The two who were arguing with the girls noticed the others approaching the Olds and left the girls to follow the others.

All six of them were large. The biggest boy was at least six feet tall and was probably a football player. His arms were massive, and his legs looked like tree trunks. He spoke first. The large brute was standing near the driver's window of the Olds.

"You guys gotta problem?" He had his hands on Scams' father's Oldsmobile.

"No. I don't have a problem," Scams replied. Scams' immediately had a dislike for the punk.

"Ain't never seen your car before. You from around here?"

The five other bullies had circled the Oldsmobile.

"What do you care?" Scams said angrily. He was thinking about Boogers.

Shooter, Axle, Baby Face and Armpits sat quietly, waiting patiently for the right time. The baseball bats and the brass knuckles were sitting on the floor at their feet.

"You gotta big mouth," the brute said while lowering his head toward Scams.

Scams could feel his body coil like a tightly wound spring; he was ready to pounce on the big ape. But he knew from experience that he had to be patient. He remained quiet.

"What would ya say if I pissed on your car?" the big brute challenged.

The other thugs laughed hysterically and pounded on the roof of the Olds. By then, the girls in the Plymouth had walked over to Scams and the others. A blonde with long hair yelled at the big boy who was confronting Scams.

"Leave them alone, Jimmy," she yelled.

"Shut up, slut," Jimmy screamed back. "Go back to the car."

"You're a creep," the blonde said, and walked back to the Plymouth, calling to her girlfriend to follow.

"You didn't answer me," the big brute said as he began to unzip his fly. His friends were laughing at what he was about to do.

"I wouldn't," Scams warned him.

"Ya know who we are faggot?" Jimmy asked, his hand still grasping his zipper.

"We're the Crusaders. And this is our area."

"I don't give a shit who you are, Jimmy. Get away from my car."

"You talk big for a guy who's sitting behind the wheel of a car. Come out here and let's see how tough you are."

Jimmy's friends were laughing at Scams and the Northsiders. They called them mama's boys and faggots. The North Side group braced for a fight.

"If I get outta this car asshole, I'm gonna rearrange your teeth as payback for what you did to my friend tonight." Scams was ready for anything.

The big kid with the tree trunk legs became quiet for a moment; his friends became quiet too. They knew what Scams was talking about.

"You mean that little faggot who sta-sta-sta-studdard?" Jimmy asked. He and his friends began laughing.

Scams tightened his grip on the steering wheel. He was filled with rage. He remembered Boogers' face and head and how badly he had been beaten. His anger peaked.

"What? You want some of me faggot?" Jimmy asked as he pounded the roof of the Oldsmobile.

It was time. Scams had had enough.

"Yea Jimmy. Just me and you. It'll be payback for my friend. But it's gotta be just me and you?"

The big thug was leaning on the driver's side door. He told Scams that it would be a fight between just the two of them. He turned away and told his gang members to "leave it alone," and this was going be an ass-kicking he was going to enjoy. As he said that, Little Nicky Scambini opened the car door with great force, slamming it into Jimmy's body. It knocked Jimmy backwards and he fell to the ground. Within seconds, Scams held Jimmy's head and neck in a headlock. It was a vise-like grip as Scams right arm tightly squeezed

Jimmy's neck. At the same time, his left fist pounded Jimmy's face. Blow after blow smashed into the bully's face.

By then, Shooter, Axle, Harry Armpits and Baby Face had gotten out of the car to watch Scams beat the large brute into submission. The North Side friends stood there with the baseball bats and brass knuckles, just in case. By the time it was over, the big bully had a broken nose and huge swollen eyes. Blood ran from his mouth and covered his face. Five-foot tall, Little Nicky Scambini did not have a scratch on him.

Later that evening, Scams and the rest of the Northsiders quietly pushed Scams' father's Oldsmobile back into the driveway of his home. But before doing so, they all came up with money to buy gas. Scams didn't want his father suspecting that he'd taken the car out. Scams' parents had not gone to bed and were still watching TV. They never found out what had happened that evening.

Nineteen

In the spring of '65, Skidmarks and Shooter joined the Air Force. Scams enlisted in the Army. I was not sure what I wanted to do. I knew that joining the Army was a possibility, but the war in Vietnam had escalated, and I felt lucky. My draft notice had not yet come my way, and I was certain that it would not.

I quit my job at the grocery store and began working at Zweigs Fruit and Vegetable Stand in Syracuse. Axle had gotten a job working there. He had become friends with the produce manager at the A&P grocery store where he'd worked. The produce manager knew the owners at Zweigs and was able to get Axle a job with them. Axle told me he was earning more money and could get me a job at Zweigs also. Scurvy Sam, Manny the Crout and his brother No-Nose also worked at Zweigs. I started to work there in August of '65. I was soon to learn, like the other Northsiders who worked at Zweigs, that I hated that job too.

Eighty-year-old "Old Man" Zweig and his fifty-year-old son Bernard owned the business. They were bossy and arrogant. They ruled the store with ridicule and sarcasm. However, there was another side to their arrogance. The two Zweigs were dunderheads, which made them easy prey for our foolish pranks. It was a way to pay them back for the way they treated us.

One of our jobs at the fruit and vegetable stand, along with waiting on customers, was to pack the fruit and vegetables in clear plastic wrap for shipping to local grocery stores. Bernard and Mr. Zweig always wanted the packages to be packed with perfect-looking produce, which they did not always have. Sometimes, the produce was not yet ripe, or it was badly bruised, or even rotten.

The job of wrapping the fruit was boring and tedious. We had to stand at a small conveyor belt that transported the produce down the line to the packer. Before wrapping the produce, we had to pick through the baskets of ripe fruit and vegetables using only the best looking pieces.

Looking for the right produce took time and was monotonous. Some of the time, Mr. Zweig or Bernard stood next to you, watching while you packed and wrapped the produce. They constantly told us that we were doing something wrong, or that we were too slow. They were a nuisance. So, at every opportunity, we would find a way to get back at them.

Axle taught me the tricks to use as payback. One way we would get back at the Zweigs was by putting rotten fruit and vegetables in the packages. We would take a rotten peach or tomato and turn the good side up in the package. That way the customer only saw the best part of the produce. Another way was to use rotten produce when we had to fill the large, bushel baskets with fruit or vegetables. To make the job go much faster, we would fill the baskets with rotten produce first and then put the good stuff on the top. Sometimes, when Axle was sweeping the concrete floor of the back room where we wrapped and packed, he would sweep up the rotten produce and throw it in the baskets.

The old man had a favorite saying, "Now cut that out." He would say those words in his high squeaky voice. "Now cut that out." "Now cut that out." After a while, Axle, Scurvy, Manny, No-Nose, and I would walk around the store repeating in high-pitched voices, "Now cut that out. Now cut that out."

We had to stock the large walk-in cooler with fresh produce that came in off the trucks every day. The temperature inside the cooler was about forty degrees. The cooler door was equipped with a lock that had to be opened with a key each time an employee went into the cooler. Old Man Zweig was paranoid about someone coming into his produce stand and stealing his goods. He installed massive dead bolts and extra locks on all of the doors. The key for the cooler door was hidden under a shelf next to the cooler. The cooler door locked automatically when the door was closed. If we had to go into the cooler for any reason, we needed to brace a piece of wood against the door to hold it open. Otherwise, the door would close behind you and you would be locked in. Once the cooler door was closed, it could not be opened from the inside. Anyone who became locked inside the cooler could scream and yell as much as they wanted, but no one would hear them.

One day, Axle was sweeping the packing room floor where the large walk-in cooler was located. He noticed Old Man Zweig inside the cooler; he was inspecting his produce. His back was to Axle, and he didn't know that Axle was sweeping the floor. Axle set aside his push broom and quietly walked toward the cooler and closed the door. He decided he would let the old man cool for a while and then nonchalantly open the door, as if he were searching for produce. Axle smiled at what he had just done. He picked up his broom and went back to sweeping the floor. Axle told no one that he had locked Old Man Zweig inside the cooler.

A few minutes later, Bernard was walking around and asking everyone if they had seen "Daddy." Fifty-year-old Bernard always called the old man, Daddy. Anyway, no one knew where the old man was. Suddenly there was a full-scale search. We looked everywhere. Even Axle put on an act and stopped sweeping the packing room floor and joined in to look for the old man.

After about twenty minutes had gone by, Bernard decided he would check the cooler. We then heard Bernard screaming in his feminine voice, "Daddy, Daddy, are you okay?" When we heard Bernard's sissy screams, we ran to the cooler. Old Man Zweig was sitting on a crate of tomatoes. He was half frozen. Bernard was trying to help him up, but the old man would not move. He just sat on that tomato crate, half frozen, and staring with a blank expression. He was shaking pretty bad too. Bernard kept yelling, "Help me with Daddy. Help me with Daddy." Axle was standing off to one side of the packing room. I could see him smiling. I knew then that Axle was involved.

After a few minutes, we managed to help Bernard lift his father off the crate of tomatoes. We walked Old Man Zweig to the packing room and had him sit down on a box of plums. Bernard asked him if he should call an ambulance, but the old man couldn't talk. His mouth was trembling and his lips were blue. But, after a few minutes, the old man had thawed out and began walking around his stand. He began yelling commands to the employees who had just saved him from going into deep freeze.

Manny and No-Nose were throwing rotten peaches at each other when Old Man Zweig caught them. "Now cut that out," he yelled at the two brothers. When he turned and walked away, Manny threw a moldy peach at No-Nose and hit him square in the face.

A few weeks later, the produce stand burned to the ground. When Old Man Zweig heard about the fire from Bernard, they raced to the site. As the old man watched his business turn to ashes, he suffered a heart attack and died. The business never re-opened. I heard that Bernard was never the same again. He became a recluse, never working another day in his life. Bernard died a few years ago. He died on the same month and the same day as "Daddy." A heart attack killed him also.

Where the produce stand used to be, there now stands an apartment building. The building houses drug addicts and prostitutes. Years ago, there were sounds of innocent laughter and tomatoes splattering against the walls of the produce stand. Today on that corner, one can hear an occasional scream of terror from an innocent victim, or the sound of a gunshot.

Twenty

By the spring of 1965, the Vietnam war had become headline news. Every day was a relentless and non-stop media blitz. More and more American soldiers were being interviewed about their experiences in the war. There was war footage filmed in black and white that showed dying soldiers, and Vietnamese villages being searched for the enemy. Young boys from all over the country were being drafted to participate in the carnage. I remained lucky; my number had not yet been called.

Axle joined the Army on July 5, 1965. He left for basic training five days later. When Axle told me he had enlisted, I became frightened. I was scared for him, and suddenly, I was scared for all of the other Northsiders who were slowly enlisting or getting drafted into the Army. I also became scared for myself.

I had always been afraid of the possibility of going off to fight in a war that I knew nothing about. I thought all the Northsiders felt as I did. When Axle told me he had joined the Army's elite, the 101st Air Borne, I told him he was crazy. I asked him why he would do something so stupid. We were sitting underneath the willow tree at Skeleton Island. The same willow tree where we had become blood brothers. It was another warm summer day. The sun was bright, white puffy clouds dotted the sky.

"You can get killed jumping out of airplanes," I told him.

"Not me, Stretch. I'll be fine." Axle had the confident look he always had. This time I didn't believe him.

"Ax, I heard that once you parachute into Vietnam and your feet hit the ground, if you live in those first 30 seconds, then you have a chance of making it through your tour."

"I'll be fine, Stretch," he kept saying.

"Yea Ax, but why are you going over there?"

Axle changed the subject. I could sense that he wanted to. He asked me something about my car. Then we ended up talking about all the fun we had that summer. We talked about Scams and Shooter and Skidmarks who were all gone. All three were in Vietnam somewhere.

Axle told me that the night he told his parents that he had enlisted, they'd both cried. It shocked Axle to see his father cry. His dad went to a corner bar and got drunk, and he stayed drunk until Axle left for basic training.

We sat beneath the shade of the large willow tree for two hours. Some moments we talked, others we became quiet. During one of the still moments, Axle broke the silence.

"Stretch, you gotta make me a promise?"

I could see that Axle wanted to say something that was important to him.

"Sure Ax, what is it?"

Axle became quiet. He looked down at the ground and stared into the dirt, as if he were searching for something. The fire we built was blazing hot. It roared in front of us. It seemed as though Axle was caught in a trance. Occasionally he glanced up at the flames leaping from the fire.

"Ax? You okay?"

"Yea." He smiled at me. "Just thinkin'."

"What was the promise, Ax?"

Axle looked at me and was quiet again. He glanced at the fire and then looked back at me.

"We're blood brothers, right?"

"Of course, Ax."

"If anything happens to me in Vietnam, Stretch. Would you make sure my body comes back home? I couldn't say anything like this to my parents."

A sick feeling grew in the pit of my stomach. I did not want to talk about what might happen to Axle. I did not want to think about it either. But, we were blood brothers; we'd made a vow to each other.

"Hey Ax, no problem."

What else can I say, I thought. I tried to sound as though I was not worried about him. I wanted to say something that seemed appropriate, but I could not find the right words.

"I keep having these bad dreams. Like I'm gonna get killed over there." Axle paused and took a deep breath. I didn't want to hear anymore. Axle was not looking at me; instead he poked a long branch into the roaring fire.

"It's like I'm gonna die, and my body will never be found so it stays in Vietnam. Then I wake up scared. My heart is racing and I'm sweating."

"Don't worry, Ax. Nothing's gonna happen to you. You're too lucky." I smiled and jabbed him in the ribs.

Axle reached into his jacket pocket and brought out the red Swiss Army knife I had given him a few short years before.

"You've never used your knife for anything, right?" Axle asked.

The knife that Axle had given me was in my trouser pocket. I removed it and held it in my hand.

"That's right, Ax. That was our promise. Never to use the knives for anything."

"I'm gonna keep this with me the whole time I'm in Vietnam, Stretch. I won't use it for nothin'."

He read the inscription out loud.

"For Dickey Axle Palumbo My Friend."

I read the inscription on my knife, "For Frankie Stretch Pandozzi My Friend."

It was time to leave. The sun was beginning to move toward the western horizon. Axle and I put the fire out and walked to where I had parked my '55 Chevy.

We talked again about our summer and about the North Side. About the girls we'd wanted to date, but never had. We reminisced about the crazy things we had done, like blowing up carp and getting drunk on church wine. And, we talked about the future. We would raise our families close to one another, so that we would be able to remain friends. But, Axle never did tell me why he'd enlisted in the Army. The next day he left for basic training.

With many of the North Side gang either away in college or in the service, I began to wonder even more about what I was going to do with my life. I became very lonely. Axle was gone and I felt empty. I tried to go carp fishing, but lost interest. I went to Skeleton Island once, but came home feeling even more depressed. I kept wondering about how Axle was. He was in Vietnam. The last letter he'd written had come from a place called Khe San.

Twenty-One

I watched the evening news every night, hoping to see Axle being interviewed by a war correspondent. And, when I said my prayers, I always included a blessing for Axle.

By the middle of '65, I'd formed two new friendships. The time I would spend with my new friends helped to fill the void left by Axle and the other Northsiders who were gone.

Carmine Supa was a Northsider. He'd graduated a few years earlier from North High School. He was skinny like I was. However, Carmine had mammoth-sized arms for his slender build. His biceps looked like large cantaloupes. He was funny and easy going. I had known Carmine for a few years on a casual basis. He used to hang out with an older cousin of mine, Benny Marrone. Benny had graduated with Carmine.

Mel Ames was the second person I made friends with. I'd also met Mel through my cousin Benny. The two of them had met at a community college in Syracuse. Mel was a great fit for Benny, Carmine and me because he was as funny and carefree as we were. Mel was also the fastest runner of our newly formed group. Carmine, Benny, and I learned of Mel's speed through our weekly touch football games. During those games, the three of us would exhaust ourselves trying to catch Mel. He loved to run with the football. He and Carmine were usually on one team and my cousin Benny and I were the other team. Sometimes we would exchange players, but it didn't matter, Mel always wanted to be the "go to" guy and either run with the ball, or have it thrown to him.

We played touch football at various parks and schools on the North Side. When we tired of the Round Top, which was the highest point at Schiller Park, we would go to Salem Hyde School, or to North High. Everywhere we went, we carried a football with us. Benny owned a white Ford Falcon. We would pile into the Falcon and drive to wherever we were going to play our games. Even though Carmine and I had cars, Benny always ended up being the designated driver.

Playing touch football was not the only recreation that Mel, Carmine, Benny and I enjoyed. Chasing after girls was also a high priority. Unfortunately, the girls were as elusive as Mel when he was running. The combined testosterone level between the four of us could have been used to launch the first Titan Two Missile. We were in heat, and in the need of relief. Every evening we would jump into Benny's Falcon and either cruise the Syracuse streets looking for easy girls, or go to one of the popular nightclubs: Bayhouth's, the Fayetteville Inn or Huit's. We would meet girls, dance with them, flirt, and then try to coerce them into the backseat of Benny's Falcon. But, it never happened. Carmine came close a few times. Mel and Benny said they did, and as for me . . . . The only time I ever saw the backseat of Benny's Falcon was when I sat in it next to Mel on the way to one of our touch football games, or when we were cruising the streets of Syracuse.

There was one time, however, after a touch football game, when Mel, Carmine, Benny and I went to a party in Syracuse, where the three of us almost got lucky. Benny had met a girl at college. She'd told him about her party and said that he could come and to bring some friends. Benny had heard that this girl was easy to get into bed, and that her parties and her girlfriends were an invitation to an orgy. When Benny told us about the party, we all became very excited, but Mel was beyond excitement. Mel was dangerous. He figured he would be able to get laid. He was in a state of white heat. Mel was at the combustible level. He thought it would be a night to remember, and it turned out to be just that.

Before the party, we each prepared ourselves for an evening of unmitigated sex. We showered longer, brushed our teeth until our gums bled, and dressed in our most impressive wardrobe. Benny wore a Sears and Roebuck outfit with matching white pants and shirt. The short-sleeved shirt had Benny's initials imprinted over the left breast. Carmine wore a pair of brand new tweed bell-bottoms and a green and gold madras shirt. I wore a pair of white bell-bottom pants and a light green, polyester shirt.

Mel was decked out in a light blue Nehru jacket, light blue polyester bell-bottom pants, and a wide-collared white polyester shirt. He wore the shirt open and unbuttoned all the way down to his navel. A large, silver St. Christopher's medal hung from his neck. The Christian medal was the largest medal any of us had ever seen. He told us it was his good luck piece.

The party was full of lively girls. They were everywhere. In fact, the only people at the house were the girls and us. Mel, Benny, Carmine and I thought that we had died and gone to heaven. Mel was the most excited, though. Within minutes of arriving at the party, Mel began chasing a giggly brunette with large breasts. He'd spotted her as soon as Benny's Falcon had pulled into the driveway.

Carmine decided to toss the football we carried with us. His target to play catch with was another brunette. She was wearing tight shorts and a very revealing halter-top. Benny honed in on the tall blonde beauty who'd invited us. I moved around from one girl to another never settling on any one in particular.

But the night ended as usual. We went home demoralized and defeated. Once again, the opposite sex had failed to give in to our advances. Our self-esteem had once again been shattered, but Mel's ego was hurting the most. Mel told us that he'd tried very hard to get the brunette with the large breasts into the upstairs bedroom. But, she'd proven to be a very difficult catch for him. They'd began by making out on the living room couch. Mel said she was a great kisser. And, when she stuck her tongue in his ear, he figured that was his cue to move her up to the bedroom. But, when he grabbed her arm and began to drag her away, she became angry. Mel told us that he'd only begged her for a little while. However, Benny, Carmine and I knew Mel better than that. We were sure that Mel had too many hands for her to handle.

By the next morning, we were feeling better and it was back to playing touch football. That was the way the rest of the summer went, as well as into 1966. Mel, Carmine, Benny and I remained close friends. But then Mel moved away, Carmine enlisted in the Army, and my cousin Benny moved to New York City. On April 7, 1966, I left Syracuse to go to basic training at Lackland Air Force Base in Texas.

Twenty-Two

The sounds of children laughing brought me back to the present. I glanced at my watch and realized that I had been sitting in the woods behind the little red house all morning. It was 12:30 p.m. and time for me to leave. As I walked down the driveway that led from the house I'd grown up in, two young Vietnamese girls ran toward me. They were both giggling as they approached. At the same time, the young Vietnamese girl who had greeted me earlier that day came out from my old house. She was still carrying the baby. She smiled at me as the two girls ran to their mother. The three hugged each other while I nodded and said thank you to the mother. I walked to my car and noticed two African American youths standing on the corner smoking cigarettes. I thought back to when I had skipped school. I remember I had never been so brazen as to stand on a street in the middle of the day when I was supposed to be in school. Truant officers roamed the area back then. If we were caught, we would be expelled from school. It was the only option. So, instead of standing on a street corner when we were supposed to be in school, we would hide at Skeleton Island, or drive around the city burning gas.

The two youths noticed me and stopped talking. One, a boy of about fourteen, stared at me. He seemed surprised at my being there in his neighborhood. The other, who looked a little older, said something to me. I ignored them and got into my car. As I did, the younger youth flicked his cigarette toward me. They laughed as I drove away.

I was hungry and decided to stop at a Vietnamese restaurant two blocks away. I had never eaten Vietnamese food and wanted to try it. When I was growing up in this North Side neighborhood, the Vietnamese restaurant used to be an Italian restaurant. An Italian immigrant owned it. His name was Antonio Di Campasse, and the restaurant was named after him.

Di Campasse's was a popular place. Mostly North Side patrons frequented the restaurant. It made no difference if you were of Italian, German or Irish heritage. Everyone felt welcome. For years, Di Campasse's was the place to go when you wanted to have a beer with friends or a dinner with the family. Everyone loved the restaurant's friendly atmosphere. Antonio and his family were always working there. Antonio was the bartender. Maria, his wife, cooked the meals and their two daughters, Anna and Rosalie, waited on tables. Decorated in an Italian atmosphere, the restaurant had large pictures of Italian lovers in gondolas, floating down the waters of Venice. On the shelves of every wall were bottles of wine. Italian music was often heard. That was because Antonio's elderly uncle Tommasso roamed the restaurant with his accordion while singing Italian verses to the customers. Everyone called Uncle Tommasso, "Zio," which is the word for uncle in Italian. Zio had a deep baritone voice, a friendly smile, and a wonderful sense of humor. When he was not singing, Zio would help with bartending or cooking. He would often say that he was not good looking enough to wait on tables; therefore, he left that job to Anna and Rosalie.

I walked into the Vietnamese restaurant and was amazed at the complete transformation that had taken place. Soft Asian music from a CD player had replaced Zio's songs. Gone were the pictures of gondolas and Italian cities. Now there were pictures of Vietnamese villages and water buffaloes. The smell of spaghetti sauce and pasta had been replaced by the distinct odor of fried egg rolls, grilled pork, hoisin sauce, and shrimp. I sat at a booth along the wall where Di Campasse's bar once stood. The restaurant was full of mainly Asian customers. For a moment, I felt as if I had taken a trip to another country. I realized again just how much the North Side had changed.

I read the Vietnamese menu, which also had a translated English version. A young Vietnamese girl took my order. She smiled at me while explaining how the food was prepared. I ordered PHO' XE LUA, which was a bowl of rice noodles in a beef broth, mixed with sliced beef sirloin, beef brisket and beef meatballs. A few minutes later, my lunch arrived. As I sat at my table reflecting on the past and eating my lunch, three loud popping sounds were heard from just outside the restaurant. Instinctively, everyone had an idea what had made the sounds. Reacting immediately, Nguyen Cuong, the owner, and his two sons ran to the doors and locked them. Many of the customers were staring out the restaurant windows, looking in the direction of a young African American girl and boy standing on the street corner. The girl was screaming hysterically. The gunshots had come from their direction.

The restaurant's customers were talking to each other in Vietnamese. Most of them had gotten up from their tables to get a better look outside. Cuong's wife, Lien, had called the police department, and within a few minutes they had arrived. A drug-related crime was apparently the motive for the shooting. Someone had fired two shots from a moving vehicle; one or both of the youths standing on the corner had been the target of the attack.

The police asked questions of everyone in the restaurant. They were trying to get a description of the car involved. While sitting in the back of the police car, both teenagers were questioned and then taken to the city police station for more information. An hour later, the restaurant had returned to its normal routine. Cuong brought me a fresh bowl of PHO' XE LUA and sat down at my table. He wanted to know what I thought of his food and how I felt about the shooting two houses away.

We talked for an hour. Cuong told me why he had come to this country and why he chose to live on Syracuse's North Side. He told me how he'd started his restaurant. He talked about his homeland of Vietnam and his family members who were still living there. I told Cuong that I had grown up in this neighborhood. And, I told him about the changes I had seen. He said the crime had become worse in recent years, and he had to move away from the city to the suburbs to get his wife and three children away from the crime. I left the restaurant feeling as though I had made a new friend, and I thought about how strange life could be.

As I drove to my home in the suburbs, I thought about how I had always viewed the Vietnamese. I had thought of them as a culture of people who ran around in black pajamas, talking in a strange voice, and killing American GIs. I'd pictured them as only eating rice and sleeping in straw huts. And, I'd never imagined that someday Vietnam would move to the North Side, or that I would be frequenting a Vietnamese restaurant that once had been an Italian eatery. From then on, each time I traveled back to the North Side, I would stop at the Vietnamese restaurant. Cuong and I would spend hours talking about his country or my old neighborhood. There was a nagging, inquisitive part of my soul that wanted to know more about the people of Vietnam and their customs.

The more I listened to Cuong, the more I needed to know. At the time, I was not sure why I had become addicted to my conversations with him. What I did understand was that our conversations pulled me toward something that needed to be known. A part of me, deep down inside my soul, was pushing upwards, wanting to be recognized. That something had always been there. In the past, I'd avoided the feelings. They had started when Heinzie was killed in Vietnam; but my meetings with Cuong intensified those feelings.

The questions of why I had become concerned about what was happening to the North Side, along with wanting to know more of the Vietnamese culture, kept me searching for the answers. Deep inside of me I knew the answers were there, and I wanted to discover them.

I once read that the Swiss psychologist and psychiatrist Carl Jung coined the word, "synchronicity." Jung's studies about the relationship of cause and effect allowed him to believe in the relationship between happenings in our lives. He believed that a chance meeting between two people happened for a reason. Jung was confident that events in our lives that appear to have no meaning do, in effect, relate to something we want, or are hoping for, even though we may not consciously know it. Was my meeting Cuong one of those strange happenings, which on the surface seem inconsequential? And, would I discover some truth about myself later on. The only thing for certain was that the North Side and its changing attitudes had a magnetic hold on me.

Twenty-Three

I had no choice. The Army sent me a draft notice and I had ten days to either enlist in the Air Force, or become an Army soldier. I chose the former. Two weeks before the draft notice had arrived I had already talked with an Air Force recruiter about enlisting. I knew my time was up. My draft number was slowly, but confidently, approaching being called. It would only be a matter of time before the Army would grab me and send me off to that place called Vietnam. But, I had another idea.

For some weeks, I had given serious thought to what career path I wanted to follow. I knew I had to hurry and make a decision; and the Army was not an option. I reasoned that if I could get training as a jet engine mechanic in the Air Force, then I would always have a job when my tour of duty was over. Airplanes had always fascinated me, and the thought of repairing their engines was intriguing.

The Air Force recruiter told me that jet engine mechanics were much needed, and my chances of getting into jet engine school were good. But, I needed to take and pass the aptitude test for jet engine mechanics. I took the test on the next day. I was then told that I would be notified of the results when I finished my basic training. The next day, I took my physical, which to my dismay, I passed. I was born with flat feet and scoliosis of the spine. These two physical problems alone were usually enough to disqualify a person for military duty. I had been hoping that I would be one of those fortunate individuals who ended up failing their physical. I wanted to go to jet engine school, but not that bad.

I had less than two weeks before I would be leaving my home on the North Side. While waiting, I became depressed. I was alone with my fears. My parents had not said much to me about my enlisting. They more or less left me alone with the choices I made about my life. My friends from the North

Side were gone. I was left alone to wait and wonder about the decision I had chosen for myself.

I spent many lonely hours driving around the North Side reminiscing. Sometimes I went bowling, or to the movies, just waiting for the day when I would leave home. Two days before I left, I sold my '55 Chevy. The dealer that I had bought it from bought it back from me.

The last two evenings at home were the hardest time. I sat in my room listening to the rock and roll stations. I wondered about whether I really would become a jet engine mechanic. And, would I end up in Vietnam anyway. In the last letter I'd received from Axle, he told me that the Air Force was in Vietnam performing many different duties. He stated that there were some large Air Force bases that were being used to support the war. Axle told me he was glad that I hadn't joined the Army. He said that the war in Vietnam was pretty bloody. And, that GIs were getting killed too easily.

I arrived at Lackland Air Force base in Texas for basic training. It did not take me long to realize that I hated basic training and despised the Air Force. In addition, when I discovered that I was being turned into a plumber, instead of a jet engine mechanic, I vowed that I would get my revenge on the Air Force, one way or another.

After going AWOL and then being busted in rank on three different occasions, the shy, skinny Italian American boy from the North Side had learned how to grow up in a hurry. While I was changing, so was the North Side. The letters I received from home told me about the families that were moving away and the businesses that were closing. Families who for years had lived on the North Side were slowly moving to the suburbs. At first, I had not given much thought to the idea of my neighbors moving away. I was more concerned with finding a way out of the Air Force and getting back to the North Side. That problem was where most of my energy was being focused at the time.

I went from Lackland Air Force base in Texas to Davis – Monthan Air Force base in Tucson, Arizona. It would be my home for the next three years and nine months. As much as I'd hated Texas, I hated Arizona even more. I was assigned to SAC (Strategic Air Command) division. My job as a plumber was to maintain the water systems of the Titan II Missiles. These nuclear missiles were scattered throughout the surrounding areas of Tucson. The missiles were housed in large facilities thousands of feet beneath the surface.

I hated being a plumber, and I hated working on the missile complex. Even though I loathed the Air Force for turning me into a plumber, and someone who worked beneath the ground like a mole, the job was, in a way, a fortunate happening. There were no Titan II missiles in Vietnam. Moreover, the Titans stateside needed to be available and staffed. At the time, the United States was concerned about Russia. So, to protect ourselves, our missiles needed to be ready, in case we were suddenly attacked by Russia's nuclear missiles. This was 1966, and just a few years earlier, the U.S. and Russia had become involved in a standoff over Cuba, which had almost catapulted the two powers into a nuclear war. That conflict was the Cuban missile crisis.

Even though the problem with Russia had been avoided, it was imperative that the United States be on guard with their missile defense system. So, I became a much-needed commodity as a plumber, here in the U.S. There was no need for me in Vietnam. And, as Axle told me in a letter, I'd lucked out.

It was no surprise to anyone that I hated the Air Force. Everyone in the plumbing shop, the refrigeration shop, the electrician shop, all of the commanders, and even the Air Policemen, who were always arresting me for breaking Air

Force rules, knew how much I despised the Air Force. Everyday I thought about going home. I wanted to be back on the North Side. I missed my home and my family. I felt secure and comfortable there. I missed being at Skeleton Island and fishing for carp. I felt that I would be happier if I were back home, even if my friends were gone. It would be much better than being stationed in the middle of a massive, sandy beach that had no water.

Early in my enlistment, I'd begun counting the days until I would be discharged and sent home. I marked each day off my calendar. The calendar was taped to the inside of my locker. I felt like a prisoner in jail who was counting the days until his punishment was finally over, and he could be set free. Many years later, I discovered that my feelings about the Air Force were due to self-pity. The reality was that I did not have it so bad. The ones who'd had every reason to hate where they were were the soldiers who had been fighting and dying in Vietnam. I was the lucky one. But at the time, I was filled with anger for having been put into a situation that was out of my control. Even so, I was learning something about myself. I was learning that not having control over a situation in my life caused me great anger. And, my anger intensified on a June day in 1966. It would become a day that I would never forget.

Twenty-Four

The tiny village of An My sat on the edge of rolling green hills. An expanse of open ground used for farming surrounded the small village. A muddy stream meandered its way alongside the eastern edge of the hamlet. In the field, both young and old were leading water buffalo that were pulling wooden carts filled with Indian corn. It was a typical hot and humid day in South Vietnam. But, eight-year-old Nguyen Cuong did not care how hot it was. In the muddy creek next to his home, young Cuong was too busy trying to catch small fish with his bare hands.

Cuong's home was just like the others. They were all built on stilts and had bamboo walls and floors, and thatched roofs. Sixty tiny homes made up the village of An My. Cuong and his brother Dung lived with their parents in one of the small huts. To Cuong, this small house was the only world he knew. He thought that everyone lived this way. Cuong loved his village and his home. He loved his family and his friends. He was carefree and roamed the hills when he was not suppose to. He knew the bad people from the North were always lurking about. Nevertheless, he did not care; he was too busy having fun chasing after fish, or helping his mother work in the fields planting and harvesting the corn. But Cuong always watched and listened whenever he was with his friends or by himself. He had become accustomed to hearing the guns being fired near his village. And, he was used to seeing the Americans carrying their guns as they walked through his tiny village. They would ask the villagers questions about the bad people from the North. Then they would search the huts in the tiny village.

Cuong thought that this was the way that everyone lived. He thought every young child's father, like his, had to leave and fight in the war. He was glad that he was not yet fourteen years of age. That age was the age he feared.

North Side Story

Fourteen was the age that his brother Dung had been when the bad people from the North, wearing their black clothes, had come into his village and grabbed him and some other boys. That was the age when you were forced to fight in a war you knew nothing about, and when you were forced to kill people you did not know.

It had been two months since the bad people had come into Cuong's village and taken his brother away. They had been in the fields harvesting the corn when a military truck drove into the village. Men with rifles jumped off the truck and ran toward the villagers, grabbing young boys and yelling, "Bao nhieu tuoi? Bao nhieu tuoi?" (How old are you?). Two soldiers ran into the field where Dung had been working. The soldiers already had Dung's name and age; they knew he was fourteen. They grabbed Dung and pulled him into the truck. Dung did not try to run. He knew that if he did, he would be shot. Cuong hugged his mother as she screamed "con trai" (son). Within minutes, Dung was sitting in the back of the truck, with an armed soldier pointing a rifle at his head.

The bad people from the North ran to each hut. They grabbed every boy age fourteen and older. Mothers screamed as their sons were pulled away from their arms. Fathers, sisters, and brothers stood by and watched helplessly. They could do nothing; if they tried to help, it would mean instant death.

Cuong wrapped his arms tightly around his mother's waist as he watched the horror taking place. He could see his brother sitting quietly in the back of the truck. Cuong could tell that his brother was afraid to move. Soon the truck was filled with boys from the village. Their families watched helplessly as the truck pulled away from the tiny village. In the distance gunfire could be heard. The villagers formed small groups and prayed that some day their sons would return safely. Cuong knew that when he became fourteen, the bad people from the North would come and take him away.

That evening Cuong thought about the terrible things that had happened to his family. His father had been gone for over a year. The South needed chien si (soldiers) to fight against the bad people from the North. He was not sure if his father was still alive. And, his brother had been taken away from him and his mother. He thought about what his mother had been telling him about the strange-looking American soldiers who were there to help his village and hoped that some day the American soldiers would kill all of the bad people. He hoped it would be soon. He already missed his brother, and he wanted to see his father again.

It was difficult for Cuong to understand why people from his country, people who looked like him, his brother, his father and the villagers, would want to kill their own kind. He could not understand why the American soldiers would help his villagers by killing the bad people from the North. As much as his mother tried to explain to him the reasons for this war in their homeland, Cuong was still confused. He tried to imagine the place where the American GIs came from. It must be nice there, he thought, because every time the GIs came into his village they would pass out candy and gum to the children. The GIs would sit the youngest children on their laps and make funny faces, causing them to laugh. Sometimes, the Americans would bring medicine for the sick and the elderly. Some day, Cuong thought, I want to visit this place called America.

As the years passed, the war in Cuong's homeland intensified. Many of the villagers had gone off to fight for the South. Many of them, including Cuong's father, had not yet returned. He was not sure if they ever would. The North Vietnamese kept coming to his village and taking away any boy age fourteen or older. Cuong was still too young to be taken away. He was glad of that. He did not want to fight for the Northern soldiers. Besides, his mother needed him to help plant and harvest the corn. The work would be too much for his aging mother to do alone.

By 1976 most of the fighting had stopped. The American soldiers had left Vietnam. However, the North Vietnamese were still coming into the villages and taking away young boys, still forcing them to fight with them. Communism was still showing its ugly teeth, and Cuong was now eighteen. A year earlier, he had managed to hide from the communist troops who had come to his tiny village. But they vowed to be back again. And, when the next time came, they would take Cuong with them. Cuong's elderly mother was still working in the fields. But, she had slowed down; her age was affecting her ability to perform the hard work. Cuong's father finally had returned from the war, but he was dying. During a battle fighting alongside the American GIs, he'd been shot twice. One bullet had entered his side and exited his back. The other bullet had entered his shoulder and smashed against bone; it remained there permanently. Infections in both wounds had taken away his strength and energy. Each day he worsened; he was dying a slow death. Cuong's brother Dung had never returned home.

One evening Cuong's parents sat down with him in their tiny bamboo hut. They told him they were concerned for his safety. The Northern soldiers would be returning, and this time they would be taking Cuong. They told him it would be best for him to leave his homeland. Cuong argued with them. He would never leave his parents behind. If he were to leave, he told them, he would take them with him.

Cuong's parents told him they were both ill and would be a burden during his travels. It would be hard enough for Cuong to travel alone. He would be traveling by foot for miles and hiding in the jungle. Then he would need to take a boat across the great sea. His parents told him of stories they had heard about starvation and death. They told him about the pirates that would board the boats and steal the passengers' possessions, and sometimes beat them to death.

Cuong's parents told him that this was a trip he must make alone.

In the spring of 1976, Cuong's parents gave him a few possessions to remember them by. They were small items that he could carry in his pockets. They gave him some money, which did not amount to much—they had very little to give away. Cuong carried some clothes and some rice wrapped inside a green GI blanket that had been given to his family by an American soldier. Cuong hugged his parents goodbye and then slung the wrapped blanket over his shoulder. He was crying as he walked out of his small village, possibly for the last time.

Twenty-Five

One afternoon as I was sitting in Cuong's restaurant eating lunch, I noticed two men installing an upgraded alarm system. Cuong told me that crime in the area had increased and he needed to protect his business. He said he might sell the restaurant because he feared for the safety of his family and his customers. I told him that both he and his culture were a positive influence on the North Side. Cuong thanked me and refilled my cup with more green tea.

Ai' joined us and they talked about the good fortune they had experienced in America and how they were glad to be raising their family in this country. They said that neither of them was happy about the rising crime rate on the North Side. However, they both knew their fortunes were better here, on the North Side, than they would have been back in their homeland.

The restaurant became busy, and Ai' and Cuong left my table to attend to their business. Again, my thoughts turned to a different time, in this very same restaurant, many years past. The memory flashed across my mind for no apparent reason. That had been happening to me quite a bit. Thoughts and memories that had been forgotten suddenly surface, as if they were letting me know they must be acknowledged. In the past, I would have pushed the thoughts aside, not allowing them to cramp the spaces of my already crowded brain. But now, I have learned to allow them to linger and to speak to me. I was remembering back to a time when Cuong's restaurant had been Di Campasse's Restaurant, owned by Antonio and Maria.

It was our Senior Prom night. I was there with Axle and Shooter and their dates. I did not have a date for the prom. I'd had a date, but had changed my mind at the last minute. Her name was Anna Leone. I knew nothing about her. Even though our senior class was quite large, I thought that I knew who most of the students were. However, Anna Leone was a stranger to me.

Axle had told me she was without a date and she was "kind of pretty." I should have known better; all of the pretty girls had dates by then. And, with just one more week before prom night, the pickings were pretty slim. Axle said she did not have a date because she was shy. Her picture was not in the yearbook, so I had no idea what Anna Leone looked like. Actually, I was not interested in going to the prom. Instead, I was planning a trout-fishing trip in the Adirondack Mountains with my cousin Benny. However, Axle talked me into calling her. There was another reason why I'd decided to go to the prom after all. Axle and Shooter needed a ride. Shooter's car had been totaled in a drag race on Pepsi Road a few weeks earlier, and Axle did not have a car. Their dates had already been chosen, and they needed someone with a car to drive them to the prom and to dinner, and then maybe afterwards parking at Crap Lake to watch the submarine races. I became the chosen one.

Without ever seeing Anna Leone, I called her on the telephone a week before the prom. I asked her if she would mind going to the dance with me. She became excited and dropped the phone. I heard her scream at her mother that she was "after-all" going to the senior prom. I felt like her savior, her knight in shining armor.

The next day, Anna went shopping with her mother to buy new shoes and a dress. When I called her that evening, she told me how excited she was, and that she could not wait to go to the prom with me. I skipped school with Axle the next two days, so I still did not see or talk to Anna Leone.

Two days before the prom, I decided to introduce myself to Anna. I thought that it would be nice if I knew a little about her before the big dance. Axle told me what lunch she took, and it happened to be the same time as mine. Axle went with me to the cafeteria to point Anna out to me. We were sitting at a table with Boogers, Shooter, Scams, and Harry Armpits.

"There she is, Stretch," Axle said.

Walking into the cafeteria was one of the ugliest girls I had ever seen. Immediately, I wanted to choke Axle.

"You told me she was kind of pretty," I whispered to Axle.

Boogers, Shooter, Scams, and Armpits were laughing. They had not known, up until then, who my prom date was.

"Ga-ga God All-All Mighty. Sh-sh she's ugly," Boogers remarked.

"You sure have good taste," Shooter said laughing.

Scams and Armpits said nothing. They didn't have to, their laughter said it all.

"She isn't that bad, Stretch," Axle said. "She needs a little work. But I'm sure on the night of the prom she'll fix up real good."

"Fix up? She needs work—you say. She needs a complete overhaul. Are you sure that's her?" I whispered.

Everyone was still laughing. I was embarrassed and scared. How can I take this girl to the prom? I thought. Then Axle waved to Anna Leone, motioning her toward our table.

"What are you doing?"

"You gotta meet her some time, Stretch."

Shooter and Scams left the table. They told me they did not want to be seen with Miss Ugly. Armpits and Boogers decided to stay for some fun.

Anna Leone was a tall girl. She was also pleasantly plump. Her face was round like a basketball, and she had buckteeth. She had short, black hair, and wore it pulled back over her ears, which was a mistake. Her ears stuck out from the sides of her head. They looked like the plastic ears that came with the Mr. Potato Head toy. Anna walked up to our table, looked at me and smiled through her buckteeth. She said hi and then something else. I was too scared to pay attention. I did not want to go to the prom with this girl. My knees began to tremble and I became angrier at Axle for having gotten me involved with her. She was uglier than the Leopard.

After we introduced ourselves, Axle left us alone. I was stuck with her and had nothing to say. Anna talked for about twenty minutes. She kept telling me how glad she was that I was taking her to the prom. I was getting sicker by the minute, so I excused myself. I told Anna I was late for class, which I always was but never cared about before. I just wanted to get out of that cafeteria and away from her.

That evening I got up the courage to call Anna. I told her my aunt and uncle from Colorado were coming to Syracuse the night of the prom. I told her my parents wanted me to stay home so my aunt and uncle could visit with me, so, I couldn't take her to the prom. I lied to Anna. I did not have any aunts or uncles living in Colorado. In fact, the only relatives who lived any distance from me lived in Rochester, New York, about a two-hour drive from my home.

Anna was crying when she hung up the telephone. And, just before the telephone went dead, I heard Anna screaming for her mother. I felt like a jerk, but in my mind, I had no other choice but to cancel my prom date with her. Anna was just too ugly for me. I did not want to be seen in public with her. I figured that in a few days, she would forget about the prom and go on with her life. Anyway, I thought, it is just a silly dance.

However, I did become the chauffeur that night. That's what Axle had called me. I drove Axle and his date Cindy Piedmont, and Shooter and his date Peggy Blanchard to the prom and then to Di Campasse's for dinner.

I sat at the same table as Axle and Shooter and their dates. Zio, uncle Tommasso, was walking from table to table playing his accordion and singing Italian love songs. It was a full restaurant that evening. Everyone was having a good time. Then Manny and No-Nose showed up with two hoods they'd befriended from Valley High on the southwest side of Syracuse. All four of them were drunk.

Manny stumbled over to our table; No-Nose and the two thugs followed. Zio sensed that trouble was about to ensue, so he quickly called for Antonio who was helping Maria in the kitchen with the cooking.

"You wen ta tha Prom wit' that creep?" Manny asked Axle's date Cindy.

"Get lost faggot," Axle snapped back.

At that moment, Antonio came to our table and told the four drunks to leave his restaurant or he would call the police. One of the punks, a short stocky boy with a crewcut and a week's growth of peach fuss on his face, told Antonio to go screw himself.

Shooter got up from the table and told all four to leave the restaurant, or else he was going to have the entire Henninger High football team, who were also present with their dates, throw them out of the restaurant. The punks from the other side of the city pushed Shooter back into his seat. The next few minutes were chaos.

The other students in the restaurant who'd come from the prom took the fastest route to help their fellow classmates; they went through, over and around the dinner tables. A wild free-for-all started, with many punches being thrown. Food and broken glass littered the floor. But, as quickly as the brawl had started, it ended. Shortly after the melee had begun, the police arrived. The two hoods from Valley High were taken to the police station. Manny and No-Nose were not to be found. Just as the fight had broken out, the two brothers decided to run and hide.

Twenty-Six

Cuong finally had made it across Vietnam to the South China Sea. It took him almost three months. During that time, he'd had to walk through the thick jungle and the tall elephant grass. He'd stopped in villages along the way, asking for directions to the great sea. He'd bought rice when he needed it. At times, he'd been given food by his sympathetic countrymen. Cuong had been told to avoid the major streets and highways because the North Vietnamese soldiers still patrolled along those routes.

By the time he reached the sea, his clothes were torn and dirty. His sandals were worn down to thin slices of broken leather. His body, face, and hands were cut and bruised from walking through the thick jungle brush. Many times, he'd thought about turning back and going home. He missed his parents and his small village of friends and neighbors. He'd wondered if his father was still alive. He'd worried about his mother's health and wanted to return to his village to help her in the fields, but he knew he could not go back. He had traveled too far to turn back. His new home was in front of him, beyond the great sea. In time, he thought to himself, I will understand why I had to make this journey.

Cuong's father had told him the name of an old woman who lived by the sea. Everyone knew her as "ba Lan" (grandmother Lan). She owned many small fishing boats, and for money, she would provide passage to Malaysia where a refugee camp had been set up. From the camp, the United States would then fly the refugees to America, where they would help them begin a new life. But Cuong had to be careful when he arrived at the great sea. There were many communist soldiers patrolling the roads along the sea. The soldiers knew that people were escaping to other countries, and they tried, with much success, to catch them.

It was evening when Cuong had snuck into the village where ba Lan lived. He'd asked the first person he saw, a fisherman, if he knew where grandmother Lan lived. The fisherman knew exactly where ba Lan's home was. He led Cuong to a small hut that was surrounded by fishing nets and small wooden boats. Cuong could smell the sea and hear the waves rolling onto the shore. It was the first time he'd been near water as vast as the sea. He could feel a sense of thrill and fear as he listened to the crashing waves.

Ba Lan was much older than Cuong had expected. Her teeth were gone, and her skin hung in loose wrinkles from her body. She was short and thin and had very large eyes. Ba Lan made Cuong feel uncomfortable. He had seen many old women before, but this woman was different from the others. He would soon find out how different.

Cuong explained to her where he had come from and what he wanted to do. The old lady understood. She had helped hundreds flee the country. She told him it would cost Cuong four hundred thousand Dong. Cuong's hopes for reaching Malaysia and the United States were destroyed. He only had four hundred and fifty thousand Dong left, and he needed to have some money left after he'd paid for the boat passage.

Cuong tried to get ba Lan to lower her price, but the old woman would not give in. "Four hundred thousand Dong," she kept yelling at him. Then she asked if he had anything to trade along with the money. Cuong told her he had nothing except the tattered clothes on his back, the dirty GI blanket, and a few small utensils used for eating. He did not tell her about the personal items in his pockets that his parents had given to him. Ba Lan unrolled the GI blanket and smiled a toothless grin. She told Cuong she would take the blanket and three hundred thousand Dong. Cuong thought for a few minutes about the old lady's offer, then he said yes and handed her the money and his GI blanket. He remembered the American GI who had given the blanket to him. He felt guilty for giving it away. Perhaps the GI will understand why I do this, Cuong thought.

Ba Lan told Cuong to be at the dock at seven o'clock the next morning. There, he would ask to meet with the fisherman Hung. Hung was the person who would take Cuong and the others to Malaysia.

That evening, Cuong slept in a small hut that was used by the old woman to store fishing gear for her boats. He walked around the small bamboo hut, looking at everything that was strange and new to him. He noticed at least a dozen GI blankets folded neatly in a corner. He smiled to himself as he thought about ba Lan's cleverness. He unrolled a blanket and within minutes was fast asleep.

The next morning, Cuong walked to the dock and located Hung the fisherman. Hung was busy loading the other thirty-eight passengers onto the tiny wooden boat. Cuong stepped onto the boat and immediately noticed how small and cramped it was. He had trouble walking between the other passengers. They were squeezed next to one another on the floor of the boat. Cuong sat down between a crying baby and a woman. He noticed how bad the boat smelled. It smelled of spoiled fish and the sea. The strong, putrid odor was making Cuong sick.

When Hung finished loading the passengers aboard the tiny boat, he told them that the trip would take about three weeks. He also told them that he could not promise they would arrive at Malaysia without any incidents. Within minutes, Hung guided the boat from the dock toward the open sea.

Cuong thought about what Hung had said. Many people had told him that the boat trip could be the most grueling part of his journey. They told him stories they had heard about the pirates from Thailand, and how they would rape and kill many of the passengers on the way to Malaysia. They'd warned him about starvation on the boats. However, Cuong had decided to take his chances; he had come too far to turn back.

With each cresting wave, the tiny boat bobbed up and down. Cuong was not used to the bouncing, nor were the other passengers. After an hour of bouncing aboard the tiny boat, many of the passengers began to lean overboard to vomit. Cuong was one of them. His stomach rolled and churned. He wondered how he could possibly survive the sea for three weeks. Again, he was not sure if he had made the right choice in leaving his home.

The tiny boat was filled with both young and old, thirty-eight refugees in all. A few babies were crying, and their mothers tried to keep them comfortable. Cuong watched a family of five huddle together in the corner of the boat. The family consisted of two young boys, a young girl, and their parents. The two boys kept trying to get up and walk around the boat. Their parents kept yelling at them to sit still, or else they would fall overboard. The youngsters did not seem to care.

Cuong noticed two young girls sitting next to each other. One of the girls, a pretty girl who looked younger than the other girl, kept looking in Cuong's direction. He wondered if they were traveling together. He was lonesome and homesick and wanted to talk to the pretty girl, but he needed to get up the courage to do so. Cuong had always been too busy to talk to any of the girls in his village. He was usually in the field helping his mother plant or harvest the corn. Besides, he thought, there were no girls in the village as pretty as this one.

That evening the weather turned bad. Rain and high winds pounded the tiny boat. There was no place on the boat to go for shelter. Hung and his two crew members had the only shelter available, and they never offered to share it, not even with the oldest passengers. All night long, the rain and high winds tormented the passengers. The wet refugees, still sick from the rocking boat, leaned over the sides of the boat to vomit. The two babies cried continuously. Cuong felt helpless and wanted to help them. He thought about asking

Hung to help the elderly and the babies. Maybe, a warm blanket or a space beneath the roof, he thought. But, his better judgement told him that he should not offer any advice to Hung. He did not trust the fisherman.

By early next morning, the winds had died and the rain had stopped. The sky was clear and the sun was beginning to rise. Most everyone was asleep. No one had had much sleep during the night. Cuong stood up and looked out over the vast South China Sea. He saw nothing but a flat surface of calm water. He marveled at the difference in the sea from one day to another. Just a few hours ago, it had been a raging and unforgiving turbulence; yet now the sea was peaceful and calm.

Cuong watched the other passengers beginning to awaken. The two babies began to cry. They must be very hungry Cuong thought. No one had eaten much since boarding the small boat the previous morning. What food there was in their bodies had been lost when they became sick and vomited. None of the passengers had brought much food with them. Most of them had had to make long journeys to the sea, like Cuong. They'd needed to travel lightly, buying food as they'd moved from village to village.

Hung and his crew had not offered much food, just a few ounces of rice for each passenger. Cuong was upset at the way that Hung and the other two boatmen treated the passengers. He looked toward the small shack where Hung and his crew had stayed all evening during the rainstorm. They were drinking tea and eating a morning breakfast of eggs and fruit. The crew was laughing and having a good time. They seemed to care very little about their passengers.

Cuong could see that the two young girls were awake. The pretty girl looked at Cuong and smiled. He blushed slightly and smiled back. By midday, the sun had become hot, as the tiny wooden boat moved closer to freedom. Most of the passengers felt better. Their stomachs had become accustomed to the rocking boat. Everyone was beginning to get hungry, and each refugee ate bits and pieces of the little food they had brought with them. Cuong was eating dried noodles that he had purchased from ba Lan.

The two young girls sat close together. They watched the other passengers eating their small portions of food. Cuong wondered if they had any food. He'd discovered that the two girls were traveling alone. They kept to themselves and spoke to no one. Cuong wondered if he should offer them some of his dried noodles. The pretty girl looked his way and smiled again. That smile was all he needed. He decided to make his way over to where they were sitting.

"Would you like some dried noodles?" Cuong asked.

The older girl shook her head no. The young pretty girl smiled and said yes. Cuong handed her the small bag of noodles, and she stood up to take it. He noticed how pretty she was. As she stood next to him, he could see that she was even more lovely. Her hair was very long and ebony black. She smiled at Cuong as she ate some of the dried noodles.

They sat down, squeezed next to each other. The older girl seemed upset that Cuong had moved in so close to them. He held the bag of dried noodles toward her, but again she refused. Within a few minutes, Cuong and the young girl were talking freely. She said her name was Tang Ai'. Her older sister's name was Bian. They had traveled from a small village near Saigon. The two sisters had arrived at the boat alone. Their parents had been killed by the communists because their brother had tried resisting their demands to join their cause. Ai' was seventeen and Bian was twenty-three. They were both going to America.

Cuong enjoyed talking with Ai'. Her smile never left her face. And, he loved to hear her laugh. He was glad he'd made the trip. They talked for hours. However, Bian never said a word. Occasionally, she would get up from the wooden floor and walk around the cramped boat to stretch her legs. She never talked to any of the passengers. Cuong thought that perhaps the older girl did not want to be part of this trip.

Cuong and Ai' spent the next two weeks sitting next to each other on the small boat. They learned about each other's families, and each other's likes and dislikes. They talked about what they wanted to do once they arrived in America. They huddled together when the seas became rough, and the wind and rain pelted the tiny boat. Bian kept to herself and seemed to distrust everyone, including Cuong.

Ai' confirmed Cuong's suspicions about Bian. She told him that Bian had not wanted to make the trip. The only reason she agreed was to protect her younger sister. Bian had told Ai' that she would never forgive Ai' for leaving their homeland, even after their parents had been killed by the communists. Ai' hoped that once they reached America, Bian would once again be the kind and friendly person she once was.

As the days passed by, more and more of the passengers became sick from the lack of food and water. All of the provisions that they had brought with them were gone. Hung and his crew ate well, but never offered any of their food to the starving passengers. The water that had been given to them amounted to only a few ounces each day. The two babies had stopped crying. They were too sick and weak from starvation. Many of the passengers stopped talking; they had lost their energy to do so.

Hung told the passengers that the trip would take at least another week. Cuong was also feeling weak, but he worried more about Ai'. She'd lost her smile and would no longer talk to Cuong. When he asked her how she was feeling, Ai' responded by just nodding her head. Even Bian, who was also very weak, had tried to get Ai' to stay positive, but all hope for her seemed to be fading. Cuong begged Hung to give some food to Ai, to the babies and the older passengers. But Hung threatened to throw Cuong off his boat, into the deep sea, if he mentioned food or water to him again. Cuong worried if anyone on the boat, besides Hung and his crew, would ever reach Malaysia alive.

Twenty-Seven

People began to die. Their bodies were tossed into the sea. Cuong counted those still left alive. Of the thirty-eight who had boarded the tiny boat a month before, only twenty-one were still alive. Hung and his crew continued to do nothing to help the starving and sick passengers. When the crew themselves became low on food, they caught fish and ate them in front of their starving passengers. Cuong hated Hung more with each passing hour. If he had the strength, he would have grabbed Hung and thrown him overboard, just like Hung and the crew were doing with their dead passengers.

Cuong was very weak, but he was more concerned about Ai'. Every day she became weaker; her will to live was gone. The only food she had eaten was a small portion of rice a few days before. Hung had stopped the tiny boat at a small island in the South China Sea where he and his crew had purchased a small supply of rice and water. The rations were handed out to the passengers in tiny portions. Unfortunately, it was too late as most of the refugees were too weak and sick to eat.

Bian was more alert than her sister and she tried to keep Ai' shaded from the hot sun. The bright sun beat down on the tiny boat day after day. The only ones who had any type of cover from the sun's scorching rays were Hung and his crew. Bian hated them as much as Cuong did.

More and more, Cuong thought about his small village and his mother and father. He wondered how they were doing, and if they thought about him. Cuong's doubts about the journey became stronger. He questioned himself constantly for leaving home. He was no longer sure if the pain and suffering were worth it. Confused and weakened from hunger, he wondered if America really was the land of the free. Could the great land be nothing more than a country of deceit? Cuong's only ideas about America came from stories he'd heard from his fellow citizens. But, not one of those storytellers had ever been to America.

The hours passed slowly for the passengers on the tiny boat. Sleep was the only alternative to just sitting on the boat's wooden deck and thinking about what the future might hold. For most of the refugees, the thought of a sound sleep that passed into death was a comfortable idea. A few weeks ago, the idea of dying from starvation and then being thrown overboard into the sea was a terrible thought. But, the pains from starvation and sickness and malnutrition seemed more terrible than death itself. For some of them, death seemed a comfort.

Ai's face was sunburned. Her cheeks were swollen and red. Her lips had cracked open and bled constantly. She slept all day, only waking occasionally to moan and whisper incoherent words. Cuong was sure that Ai' would be dead by the end of the day. His energy was gone, but he managed to wipe the perspiration from Ai's face and neck, using his shirt that he had removed from his sun-baked body. The sun had roasted his skin to a burnt red. His body had also blistered and oozed puss from large swollen areas. Although he knew he needed to wear his shirt to keep the sun's rays from further burning his skin, it was the only material available for wiping Ai's face.

There was no way to cool the bodies of the dying passengers. Although the tiny fishing boat bounced around upon a sea of water, the salt from the ocean was more of a threat than a cure for the refugees aboard. Salt water on open sores caused the blisters to swell and become more painful. When the sea became rough and the small boat rocked on its waves, the passengers, with their skin burned from the sun's rays, cried in pain as the saltwater splashed their bodies.

Most of the passengers' tongues had become black and swollen from the lack of water. Hung and his crew still refused to give the refugees fresh water. Some of them had tried to drink the seawater, but they were restrained by the ones who knew better. Drinking seawater only speeded the dehydration of the dying passengers.

Bian would sleep for a few hours and then wake to care for Ai'. She would wipe her sister's face with Cuong's ragged shirt. Bian, like Cuong, also realized that Ai' was dying. As Bian looked around the tiny boat and listened to the crying and moaning of the others, she knew that unless there was another island nearby with food and water, not many of the passengers would leave the tiny boat alive. All of the elderly passengers and both of the babies had died. The only refugees still barely alive were those who had begun the trip being the healthiest. But even the strongest bodies were wasting away.

Hung seemed to delight in tossing the dead over the sides of his boat. He and his crew showed no remorse in performing the task. When death took a passenger's life, Hung and a crewmember would nonchalantly walk to the body, pick it up, and throw it into the sea, as if it were the guts from some fish they had caught. Sometimes, they would laugh at the body as they dropped it over the side of the boat. Bian made a promise to herself that if she lived through the ordeal she would somehow make Hung pay for his cruelty. It was the hate she had for Hung that drove her will to stay alive.

Five weeks from the time the tiny boat had left for Malaysia, another small island appeared on the horizon. Cuong and Bian were the only passengers alert enough to realize their fortune. Perhaps food and water would be purchased by Hung to feed the starving passengers. They fought off sleep to watch Hung and his crew guide the boat toward the small island. Cuong and Bian were filled with a cautious hope. Cautious because they knew that Hung did not care about feeding his passengers. Will he buy enough food and water to feed us? Cuong asked himself. Or, will he purchase just enough rations for himself and his crew?

Cuong and Bian noticed two wooden boats the size of Hung's approaching them. Hung and his crew steered their small vessel toward the approaching vessels. Cuong and Bian, both weakened from starvation, watched intensely as the two boats came closer and closer. Hope filled their hearts. Quite possibly, the two boats approaching them were coming with food and water. Hung and his crew began to wave toward the crews on the other boats. Cuong looked down at Ai' as she slept on the floor. She had managed to survive beyond Cuong's and Bian's expectations. Cuong wiped her brow with his shirt and believed that Ai' might possibly survive the journey. His hope lay with the two small fishing boats that were nearby. When the vessels came within ten yards of Hung's boat, ropes were passed between them. Cuong watched as the boat crews tied all three boats together as one.

There were four crewmembers on each of the boats that had come from the island. Cuong and Bian watched Hung and his crew help the eight members of the two boats onto his small vessel. Hung talked to the others as if he knew them. Cuong could not hear what they were saying. Then Cuong watched Hung take money from one of the crewmembers. Hung was excited to receive the money. He quickly stuffed the bills into his trouser pockets.

Cuong wondered why Hung was receiving money from the others. He also noticed that there was no food or provisions of any kind being brought aboard Hung's boat. If there were no provisions to bring aboard Hung's boat, why had the boats tied up with Hung. A sense of panic swept through Cuong. He was not sure why.

Hung pointed toward his dying passengers. He laughed at the remarks the others were making about the refugees. They talked for a few minutes, never taking their eyes off the dying passengers. The eight crewmembers from the other two boats walked toward Cuong and his fellow passengers.

Cuong's anxiety increased as they surveyed the sick and dying refugees. Something was not right. Suddenly Cuong's fears were realized.

The eight crewmen began picking through the pockets of the dying passengers. Most of the refugees never knew what was happening to them. The ones that knew were too sick to stop the thieves. Cuong watched helplessly as the thieving crew moved from passenger to passenger, stealing anything of value. Most of the refugees had very little with them, and any money they had was quickly taken. Also stolen were many personal items.

Cuong had heard that Thai pirates from time to time raided the refugee boats. His worst nightmare had been confirmed. He watched three of the pirates approach Bian, who was seated next to him. One of the pirates, a tall, skinny man with rotten teeth, bent over Bian and smiled at her. Bian stared back with contempt. The pirate reached down to search her pockets and Bian found enough strength to pull away, and then she spit at him.

The rotten-toothed pirate grabbed Bian and dragged her a few feet. Cuong tried to stand and go to her defense, but two pirates knocked him to the wooden floor. They told him to be still, or he would die. Cuong felt defenseless. He watched Bian struggle with the three pirates. She tried to scream but was too weak. The skinny pirate and a younger-looking boy picked Bian up and carried her to the center of the boat. Bian tried to find the strength to resist, but she was loosing the battle.

Cuong could not believe what he was witnessing. Again, he tried to stand, but was knocked down and repeatedly kicked. Hung and his crew just stood there watching. They laughed and clapped their hands as if a game were being played. Cuong was now lying on the floor, next to Ai'. His ribs were bruised from being kicking and blood flowed from his face. Ai' was sleeping and he was glad. Cuong did not want her to see the horror that was happening to her sister.

Twenty-Eight

In May of 1966, I received a letter from Axle. The letter was dated April 27, 1966; it was my birth date. Axle had not forgotten my birthday. I felt ashamed that with death all around him, Axle had still remembered my birthday while I had forgotten to send him a birthday card on his birthday, April 29. We always celebrated each other's birthdays. We'd usually celebrate by doing something stupid. On our tenth birthday, we stole Mrs. Winkle's cat and glued all four of its paws to the Winkle's front porch. When we reached our eleventh birthday, Axle and I had smoked a pack of Marlboro cigarettes. I'd taken them from my father's shirt pocket while he was in the shower. Axle and I became sick after finishing the whole pack. On our twelfth birthday, we'd hopped on a boxcar that had stopped at the candle factory. We rode in the empty car and ate sandwiches that we had brought with us. We rode the train to Rochester and back; we were gone all day. When we were thirteen, Axle and I went for a joy ride in Axle's father's '51 Ford. Axle's dad had been restoring the car; it was parked in the garage. His parents were at work and he stole the keys from his father's dresser drawer. The Ford was a stick shift, so Axle had trouble shifting through the gears as we drove around the North Side. At age fourteen, Axle and I skipped school and went fishing at Crap Lake. Two truant officers spotted us as we walked toward the lake carrying our fishing poles. We ran into the woods behind the dump and hid there until the officers gave up looking for us. At the ages of fifteen and sixteen, Axle and I drank a six-pack of Budweiser. They were six-packs that I had hidden at the grocery store where I worked. I stashed them for these special occasions. We both got drunk on two beers each.

In Axle's letter, he mentioned the war was becoming more brutal with each passing day. Many of the men in his battalion had been either badly injured or killed. He said that he could not wait for his tour in Nam to be over. He had seen enough death. That letter was to be the last one I would receive from Axle. A few weeks later, I received a telephone call at my barracks; the call was from my mother. I could tell by the sound of her voice that something was wrong. My immediate reaction was to ask her who in the family was ill, but I did not have the chance. My mother wasted no time in telling me that Axle had been killed. He'd died just two weeks before he was to be discharged from the Army and sent home.

I know my mother asked me questions. Was I all right? Could I get home for Axle's funeral? Would I go to church and pray for Axle's soul? However, I do not remember hearing them. I only remember that my body was shaking all over. I remember becoming sick to my stomach and running to the latrine to throw up. I'd hung up the phone on my poor mother without saying goodbye. When I called her back, I was still crying.

I asked my mother how much she knew about Axle's death. How was he killed? Where did he die? Was he alone? Did he suffer? My mother did not know much about the details of his death. Axle's mom had come running over to my parents' home, screaming, "My baby, my baby." She was carrying Axle's army picture.

My mother had called a priest. And, everyone had stayed with Axle's mom until his dad came home later that evening. He'd been away from home on a business trip. Not much information was given to Axle's mother about his death. That would come later.

That evening, in my calendar, I wrote a message in the June 11 square, the official date of Axle's death.

"Forever, I will remember this day.

Forever, I will remember you my friend.

Forever, we remain blood brothers."

I circled the date with a red marker and I began to cry again.

Axle's funeral was difficult. His casket remained closed, this was because of the way he had been killed. The details of his death were sketchy. The stories behind the story were passed from one person to another, but no one knew for sure exactly how Axle had died. Apparently, he'd been wounded numerous times while trying to save his platoon leader.

Axle and his platoon had been under heavy direct fire from the Vietcong, and their position was being overrun. His platoon leader had been shot in both legs while directing his unit. Axle had picked him up and thrown him over his shoulder. He was running toward cover when Vietcong soldiers began to shoot Axle from close range. Axle and his platoon leader died instantly.

I stayed home on leave for a week. It was the loneliest week I had ever experienced. I hated being back on the North Side knowing that Axle would never again be there. I tried to remain busy, but the memory of Axle was too painful. I could not function mentally or physically. I was having a difficult time trying to understand why he'd been killed. I knew there was a war and that people died in wars. But why Axle? My thoughts drifted back to Heinzie as well. I tried to understand that no one who fights in a war is immune to its terrible outcome.

I kept telling myself, in hopes that it would lessen my pain, that Axle had known he was taking a risk. He'd known that Vietnam was where every young boy seemed to be heading. Maybe the war was a game to Axle. Maybe he thought he was playing a game of war, like we used to do on the North Side. Perhaps he thought he was invincible by joining the Army's elite 101st Airborne. Axle always took chances. And, he had always been lucky. Perhaps he thought that his luck would continue in a real war.

I also realized that I was angry at Axle. I was angry because he'd become involved in a war that had become a game—a game of chess. It was being played between politicians and the Army's top brass. So, I was angry at

Axle for having wanted to become a pawn in the chess match.

More importantly, I was also feeling ashamed for not being there to help him. We were blood brothers, I told him one evening in a prayer. We promised each other that we would be there when one of us needed help, and I was not there to help you, Ax. Perhaps, I should have joined the Army with you. I could have tried to join with you on the buddy system. Maybe, if I had been with you in that ambush, I could have killed the enemy before they killed you. The guilt I felt for not being with Axle consumed me day and night. It would take a very long time before I began to understand my pain.

As much as I hated the Air Force, and being away from the North Side, I could not wait to get back to Arizona. I needed to step away from the grief I was feeling. The North Side was too close to my pain. Every time I looked out from the windows of my home, I could see Axle's house, and I would remember the times we had shared together.

In church, there was a mass for Axle, and during the mass, I remembered the times we had skipped church and gone to the drugstore to drink malts and look at girly magazines. There was too much pain for me at home, so I went back to Tucson two days early.

Back on the Air Force Base, I cared about nothing. I was insubordinate to officers, and I objected to every job I was sent out to do at the missile sites. I broke rules, fought with my superiors, and laughed at the Air Force protocol. I hated the Vietnamese, the war in Vietnam and my life in general. On three different occasions, I was stripped of my rank, busted down to no stripes. I went AWOL. I stole an Air Force truck and went on a joy ride in the deserts of Tucson, while drinking two six-packs of Coors.

No longer was I the shy introvert who'd grown up knowing nothing about life outside the North Side of Syracuse. I suddenly metamorphosed into a person who was impetuous and boisterous. I wanted to run away and hide in Alaska. Maybe up there, I thought, in the wilderness, all alone, I can forget. I went AWOL again. I did not care. I cared about nothing.

But that was a long time ago. I was young, naive, and angry. By the time I was discharged in January of 1970, my pain over Axle's death had diminished, but Axle was never forgotten. I went back to the North Side and tried to regain the youth and innocence I had known there. But I soon discovered that the North Side, like me, had begun a transformation.

The changes taking place on the North Side were different than what I ever could have imagined. I did not like what I saw. I was uncomfortable with the unsettled feeling in the neighborhoods. By the mid 1970s, my family and myself, by then married, had moved to the suburbs. And, as more and more of the first and second generation Northsiders moved away, they were replaced by a different kind of immigrant. Some of the newly transplanted Northsiders had moved from low-income, crime-ridden neighborhoods of Syracuse. While others were Asian immigrants who were escaping the rules of their communist native country.

I did not want to see the North Side transformed into anything other than what it had been, that is, full of hard-working middle-class families who respected their families, their property, and their God. It was not up to me, however, to prevent the changes that were occurring in my old neighborhood. The new immigrants would have to be the ones to lead the way. And, these new immigrants were from the very same culture I had learned to hate a few years earlier.

Twenty-Nine

As the years passed, more and more hard-working North Side families moved away. Slumlords purchased their homes and rented them to families on welfare. The clean streets that the Back Alley boys and the Northsiders used for playing touch football were filled with broken whiskey bottles and shell casings from spent bullets. During my youth, the North Side churches were always opened to the public. Anyone could stop by and light candles, or pray. Suddenly, the new occupants of the North Side began to steal the church possessions, and one by one, the doors of the churches had to be locked and bolted shut.

To claim that there was no crime on the North Side when I was growing up would be a lie. However, the crimes we committed as adolescents paled in comparison to the current crimes. Drinking the church wine and getting drunk only harmed Axle and me. Gluing the paws of a cat to a porch did not cause harm, except for a small bit of trauma for both the cat and Mrs. Winkle. And, when Axle dropped a brick on the top of Manny the Crout's head from the roof of his home, it only caused a bump on Manny's head and a trip to the emergency room.

But, when a postal carrier is robbed of his mail and then beaten with a cast iron pipe, that is when the crime becomes more than just amusement. Or, when a teacher is raped in her own classroom while students stand by and watch, that is sheer brutality.

When we were kids, we carried slingshots. Axle carved his weapon from the branch of a maple tree. I purchased mine at Woolworth's Five and Dime. Today's Northsiders carry guns. Our slingshots were used to shoot at squirrels and pigeons. Glass marbles were our ammunition. Today, the Northsiders shoot each other with real guns. Our pocketknives were used to slice open the bellies of the fish we caught, or to carve wooden whistles from tree branches.

The knives used by the Northsiders today have five-inch blades and are used to rip open the skin of one another.

"Our school teachers are mean," we used to tell our parents. When Mrs. Kowlinski slapped my face in the fourth grade because I laughed at Benjamin Cromp for pissing his pants in class, I was reprimanded. When my mother found out what had happened, she also slapped me. And, when my father came home from work, he slapped me again. Not long ago a fourth grade boy from the North Side pulled a handgun on his teacher because the teacher had slapped him. The boy's parents are suing the school.

There are North Sides everywhere, in major cities all across America, and they are changing also. The world changes every day. Countries grow and evolve, or they weaken and become consumed by much stronger countries. New medicines that cure disease are patented. Cars become sleeker and airplanes fly faster; old age is being enhanced; and businesses are moving into homes. The food we eat is being tested for better quality; architects are building taller skyscrapers; and the world of sports has become big business. I should expect the North Side to change as well.

I should not become alarmed when I see the foundation that once held a strong and proud neighborhood crumble under neglect. However, I do become saddened for the disregard for the quality of life that once had existed in the North Side. Perhaps I feel this way because a part of me has never left the North Side. I may never find the answer to the romanticism with which I view the neighborhood. But, I do know that ever since Axle's death, I have been preoccupied with this feeling of melancholy. There is a sadness that I cannot shake. It has been with me ever since I received the phone call from my mother about Axle's death. Sometimes, I feel that the death of Axle and the death of the North Side are interwoven. Perhaps, there was some sort of magical bond between Axle, myself, and the North Side, and that bond was torn apart by death.

Thirty

Bian had passed out, but that did not stop the pirates from raping her. Cuong watched in horror, as one by one, the pirates used Bian's defenseless body. When they were finished with her, the pirates laughed and joked about what they had just done. Hung and his crew were laughing also; they never tried to stop the savages.

Cuong's anger was at a fever pitch, but he could do nothing. He felt helpless. He wanted to get up and help Bian, but he knew that in his weakened condition, he was no match for the pirates. All he could do was sit on the boat deck and watch in disgust.

Ai' continued to sleep and Cuong was glad. Had she witnessed what had happened to her sister, Cuong believed it would have killed her for sure. For the most part, the passengers had been too sick from starvation to watch. They also had passed out from hunger and starvation. Cuong himself was close to slipping into unconsciousness, but fought the urge with all of his will. He needed to stay awake for Ai'. She needed his help, and he would not give in to death just yet.

The pirates walked to Bian's body. As she lay on the floor of the boat, the skinny pirate kicked her in the side. The pirates laughed. He kicked her again, and then another pirate kicked her. Soon, all eight of the pirates were kicking and laughing at Bian. Hung and his crew continued to watch. Then, Hung and his crew began passing money between themselves, as if they were taking bets.

Suddenly, Bian opened her eyes; Hung cheered and clapped his hands. He then smiled and collected money from his two reluctant crewmembers. Cuong became even more sickened as he watched Hung collect his bet. He looked at Bian and saw that she was in pain and crying. He tried to stand, but two pirates noticed and began to kick him in his face and head.

Blood rolled down Cuong's head. It poured into his eyes as he tried to watch what the pirates were doing. Bian continued to cry in pain as the skinny, rotten-toothed pirate and two others began talking. Cuong could not hear their voices, but he sensed that something else was about to happen.

As Bian lay on the floor moaning in pain, Cuong watched the skinny, rotten-toothed pirate and two others pick up Bian's limp body. Without hesitation, they carried her to the side of the boat. Bian realized in an instant what was about to happen to her. As she was being lifted above the sea, she tried to call Ai's name, but it was too late. Her body slammed into the water. The only words heard were the words of the cheering pirates and Hung's crew.

Cuong could not believe what he had just witnessed. Anger raged throughout his body. If he lived through this ordeal, he promised Bian and Ai, he would make the pirates and Hung pay for the death of Bian, and the others.

Cuong noticed Ai' beginning to wake up. He was suddenly filled with remorse. How could he explain to her what had just happened to Bian? How could he ever explain what he had witnessed?

The Thai pirates returned to their two boats and within minutes were on their way back toward the island they had come from. Cuong wondered how much longer it would be before another island appeared. The remaining passengers needed food and water. They had lived longer than Cuong had expected. He was not so much worried for his own life as he was for Ai's. He prayed for Ai' and for Bian and then drifted into sleep.

He awoke to the voices of Hung and his crew. They had thrown the bodies of three more refugees into the sea. The number of passengers barely alive was down to twelve.

Cuong watched as Hung walked from passenger to passenger, checking them for any signs of life. When he approached Cuong, he told him that he might be one of the lucky ones, and he pointed toward the open sea. Cuong managed to pull himself up by grasping onto the sides of the boat. His eyes were puffy from the beating he had endured from the pirates. He tried staring out toward the horizon where Hung had pointed. In the distance, Cuong could see an island. It was barely visible. He stared at the island for a few minutes, making sure that he was not hallucinating. When he was sure of what he saw, Cuong lay back down on the deck. Hung told him the island was called Pulau Bidong, and it was part of Malaysia.

Hung told Cuong that Pulau Bidong had a refugee camp and that was where Cuong and the other passengers were to be dropped off. He told him they would be there in a few hours. Cuong could not believe that his long journey was finally ending. He looked at Ai', who was asleep. She appeared not to be breathing; he panicked and laid his ear on her chest. He could feel the faint beat of her heart and prayed that she would hold on for just a few more hours.

Hung and his crew began to do something that they had not done in weeks. They began to pass out small portions of rice and water to the dying passengers. Cuong hated Hung, and to see him give food to the sick refugees just hours before they would be on land angered Cuong even more. He understood Hung's reasons for passing out food were selfish ones. Hung obviously wanted to appear to the islanders to be a concerned captain of his passengers. However, Cuong had other ideas for Hung. He had made a promise to Bian and Ai' that if he lived through their ordeal, he would make sure that Hung, his crew, and the pirates would pay for their crimes.

About half of the remaining passengers were able to eat, or drink the water that Hung offered to them. The others were either asleep, or only semi-conscious, staring off into the distance, not aware that their trip would soon be over.

   Cuong tried to wake Ai'; he wanted her to drink some water. After a few minutes, she began to move her lips. She managed a few swallows of water from a tin cup that Hung had given to him. Cuong wet his shirt and cleaned Ai's burnt lips and face. She tried to smile and reached for the wet shirt. The wetness was a welcome relief to her warm skin. She began licking the wet shirt, and then Ai' opened her eyes.

   Cuong smiled and tried talking to her, but she was not responding to his words. She only wanted to taste more of the water. Cuong held her head in his arms and moistened her lips. He watched Hung and his crew try to feed the other passengers. It angered Cuong to see their deceitful remorse. They care nothing about the passengers, he thought. To Hung and his crew, the refugees were no better than the fish they caught, a commodity to be sold by the pound.

   Cuong ate his portion of the rice. He needed to be as strong as possible. Once he set foot on the island, he needed his strength for Ai'. She was alone now, and Cuong still had to tell her about Bian's death. He did not cherish that thought. He had no idea how he would tell Ai' about her sister. He had never been in such a situation before. He realized how much he had grown up in the past few months since leaving his small village. And now, he would have the responsibility of telling Ai' about her sister. He wished that his mother or father were with him now. At least they would know how to break the bad news.

   Cuong realized that his entire trip had been an experience he never dreamed would happen. And, as he looked at his sick and dying fellow passengers, he wondered if any of them had thought that they would have endured so much pain and suffering. Most of the refugees left aboard the tiny fishing boat had lost a family member to starvation. Some had lost their entire family. Cuong remembered the names of every person who had died. Each time he remembered a name, he became more angered at Hung for allowing the death to happen.

Cuong had hoped that he would see no more death and evil once he left his country. He had witnessed enough death from the communists who had come into his village. Again, he wondered if death and evil were everywhere, even in America. He wanted to believe that his trip and the suffering he'd endured were worth the risk he had taken. If they were then he would make sure that the lives of those who had died aboard the tiny boat were remembered. He felt obligated toward them. He was sure that if he survived, it was because of God's will, and that God had made him the messenger for all to remember. How that was to be, he was not yet certain. Cuong only knew that he must first stay strong and keep his mind free of any sadness that he might feel. He needed to reach Malaysia, and then America, and Ai' would be his first responsibility.

The sun's rays beat down incessantly on the refugees. Again, Cuong wiped Ai's face with the wet shirt. Then he reached up and grabbed onto the side of the boat. He looked off into the distance. The Malaysian island appeared closer, and Cuong felt a rush of joy. He could see that this island was different from the others. He could begin to see the many shelters that housed the refugees. He watched as small boats moved to and from the island, perhaps carrying more refugees and supplies to the boat people living there.

Hung's tiny fishing boat moved closer to the island. Hung and one crewmember began to prepare the passengers for their departure from his boat. Hung seemed anxious to get them off his boat and into the hands of someone else.

Cuong tried to tell Ai' where they were, but she had passed out once again. He hoped that a doctor would immediately come to their aid. He knew that Ai' could die at any moment, and he prayed for her health to return. As the boat approached the island, Cuong studied its shores. He was looking for any signs that might indicate trouble. But he saw nothing to cause him concern. He wanted to believe that his troubles were over, and this was the beginning of a better life for him. However, deep down inside, Cuong was not sure what to expect on the island of Pulau Bidong.

Thirty-One

I ran into Shooter a few years after being discharged from the Air Force. I was a bartender at a tavern in Syracuse, and Shooter came in for a beer. I had taken the bartending job as a part-time job. I was also attending a local community college. I did manage to get my GED high school diploma while still in the Air Force.

The beer joint was located on the North Side. It was a real man's bar. Women were allowed, but they were afraid to come in. The tavern really had nothing women wanted. Ernie's bar was a beer and shot of whiskey kind of place. No fancy mixed drinks were made. If someone asked for a Whiskey Sour or a Bloody Mary, I would tell them that they were in the wrong place. Usually, it would be a new customer, or a woman, if she was brave enough to come to Ernie's. The owner of the bar, Henry Olsen, also known as Hank, figured that it was a waste of time to mix a drink. It was much quicker just to pour a glass of beer, or a shot of whiskey.

Most of the men who drank at Ernie's were nice guys. They enjoyed a place where they could be themselves, without women being offended. It was nothing to see customers spit on the floor; or belch and pass gas after guzzling a brew. Hank enjoyed the belching. He figured that if a guy was belching, then he was enjoying the beer. Hank also loved to drink.

Hank had opened for business about the time that I was hired. I once asked him why he'd named the bar "Ernie's Bar," and he told me it was because if a customer had a problem with the service, he would tell him to go and take it up with Ernie. Hank put up signs on the walls that read, "Have a problem with this place? Go see Ernie." Another sign read, "If you can't get in touch with Ernie, that means he's on vacation."

Shooter had heard that I was a bartender at Ernie's, so he stopped in to see me. I was shocked when he walked in the door. It had been seven or eight years since I had last seen him. He had changed quite a bit. He weighed much more than during our school years. His hair had thinned, and it was already beginning to show some gray. Shooter looked much older than he was.

He stayed at Ernie's for a few hours. He drank Peppermint Schnapps and chased it down with Budweiser beer. He told me he was working at a Chrysler automotive plant in Syracuse, and he had an apartment in the suburbs. His wife had divorced him a few years earlier. We talked about the North Side, and how it was changing. We exchanged memories of the times we had spent together. When my shift was over, I drove us to Di Campasse's where we could continue our conversation about the North Side.

We drank beer at the bar, and then had a meal of linguine with white clam sauce. After our meal, we went back to the bar for a nightcap. Shooter talked about prom night, flipping coins behind the old brewery, and our baseball games. Then he got drunk and began to get angry at things I said. When I mentioned Axle's name, Shooter told me never to mention his name to him again. When I asked him why not, he became more irritated. He told me never to mention Axle's name to him again. I never pressured Shooter as to why he didn't want me to talk about Axle. People handle grief in different ways, and perhaps this was the way that Shooter handled Axle's death. At the end of the evening, I drove him to his apartment. I have not seen him since.

At our high school reunion that same year, I saw Harry Armpits and Skidmarks. Armpits no longer had long arms. His body had grown and caught up with his arms. He was no longer known as Armpits either. Skidmarks had cleaned up his act, and Jimmy "The Skidmarks" Bartolo had become James Bartolo, Attorney-At-Law.

North Side Story

It's strange how people you once identified with can suddenly become a stranger to you. James Bartolo hardly cared that I was at the reunion. Perhaps he had forgotten that at one time we had been Northside friends and part of "The Back Alley Boys." He was a lawyer, and I was just a bartender. It became apparent to me that he was more comfortable sipping martinis with Edward Young, whom Skidmarks had hated in high school, but who was now Dr. Edward Young. I left his table and joined Harry.

Harry told me that Little Nicky "Scams" Scambini had "gone whacko." After being discharged from the Army in '69, having served two tours of duty in Vietnam, where he had received a few medals for bravery, he'd apparently had enough. The war had taken its toll on him. Harry told me that Scams had only been back on the North Side for a few months when he got involved with drugs and the wrong crowd. He'd been in a few fights and been put in jail on assault charges.

One day, Scams pulled a loaded revolver on a bouncer in The Candy Land. The Candy Land was a go-go club that featured beautiful girls dancing topless. Scams had become drunk and disorderly with one of the dancers. When the bouncer told him to leave, Little Nicky had pointed the gun at him. He told the bouncer, "I'm gonna blow your damn head off. Like I did those dinks in Vietnam."

The police came and took Scams to jail; it was his third time in jail since being discharged. When he was released on bail, pending a court date, he ran off. Apparently, he has vanished from the face of the earth. His family says that they don't know where he is. However, Harry told me that he had heard from others that Scams is hiding out in the mountains of Oregon. Harry thinks that Scams lives like a hermit off the land. It is hard for any of us to believe that Little Nicky Scambini is living with the grizzlies and eating roots to survive.

A few years ago, I was in downtown Syracuse on business. I had stopped for lunch and a beer at a local pub. Just as I was getting ready to leave, a homeless man came stumbling in. He was dirty and smelled like urine. He was wearing an old, dirt-stained Boston Red Sox baseball cap. His nose was caked with dried snot. I was shocked when I discovered that it was Boogers. Freeman Polanski was begging for money.

The owner of the pub tried to throw Boogers out the door. But Boogers fell on the floor, and began stuttering, no one could understand him. I immediately went to his aid. I told the pub owner that I would help Boogers get outside. I bought my old friend a Pepsi and a tuna sandwich. I was not sure how long it had been since he had eaten last.

I helped him walk to a bench at a bus stop. He stopped stuttering and devoured the sandwich and Pepsi. Boogers did not remember me. I tried explaining who I was and where I'd gone to school, but Boogers just stared through me. I asked him if he remembered Shooter, Scams, Armpits, No-Nose, Manny the Crout, Skidmarks, Baby Face and, of course, Axle. But Boogers seemed oblivious to me and the names I had mentioned. When he had finished eating, he remained quiet. I asked him where he lived. He said nothing. He just continued to stare at me. I was late for my appointment, so I asked Boogers if he wanted me to take him somewhere. But he still remained silent. I put a twenty-dollar bill into his hand. Then, Freeman Polanski smiled. Whenever I am in downtown Syracuse, I look for Freeman. He appears in different areas, always dirty, and always wearing his Boston Red Sox cap. I always give him money. But, he still does not remember me.

Every now and then, I take time to remember Axle. I try to give him some time in my heart. And, while I am remembering him, I wonder what kind of a person Axle would have become. I often picture him as a married man, a father with children, and a hard worker. Axle probably would have been a police officer. He often joked that he would make a good cop because he had experience being chased by them. He figured that experience would help him understand the job better.

I think that Axle would have always been a little crazy too. He would have been a great friend to drink beer with at Ernie's. Axle and I probably would have spent many summer days fishing. Our wives probably would have been great friends. And our children would have been chasing after each other, just like Axle and I had done as kids. I think about that a lot.

Thirty-Two

The Island of Pulau Bidong was just a few hundred feet from the small fishing boat. Cuong could see the shoreline. It was littered with broken pieces of boats. Chunks of wood and debris floated on top of the water. Hung told Cuong how lucky he was to have survived the long boat trip. He pointed to the wrecked boats along the shoreline and told Cuong those were what was left of the boats that had not made it to the island. Cuong noticed the sarcasm. He will pay for the lives of those who have died, Cuong thought to himself.

Hung and his crew guided the small boat onto the beach. Cuong watched a group of people walk toward the boat. As they approached, they waved to Hung. Cuong was a little concerned and wondered if Hung was friends with the islanders. If so, it would be difficult for Cuong to prove Hung's guilt. He hoped that would not be the case. Now that he was on the island of Pulau Bidong, he needed to find the right people who could help him. Ai' needed medical attention. He would help take care of her first and then deal with Hung. He prayed and thanked God for bringing him to the island. Now he asked God for help with Ai'.

Cuong could barely walk. He was helped by a young boy about his age. Two others carried Ai' to a shelter near the beach. The shelter was an old, wooden fishing boat. It had once been used by previous refugees on their voyage to Pulau Bidong. Cuong noticed that most of the scattered shelters being used as homes had, at one time, been boats. The wooden boats were lined up along the island perimeter. They housed refugee families of all sizes. As Cuong sat on a dirty mattress, sipping water that the young boy had given to him, he wondered how long the refugees had lived there. Many of the boat-homes had small gardens in front of them. Clothes that had been washed in the seawater were hanging on makeshift clotheslines. The lines had been strung using the rope from fishing nets. Cuong had many questions, but first he wanted to know where Ai' had been taken.

Of the thirty-eight people who had started the voyage with Cuong, only ten had survived. The few remaining survivors were either carried to a small makeshift hospital, or placed in various refugee boat-homes. They would be nursed back to health and then given jobs on the island, until their final flight to America.

Many of the refugees on Pulau Bidong were employed as laborers, and they were paid with food. The jobs consisted of working in the fields, growing and harvesting the food that was needed to feed the refugees. Other jobs on the island consisted of working in the offices of the immigration officials, the United Nations High Commissioner for Refugees, UNHCR. The refugees would help with tasks like processing new refugees onto the island, or helping with the paperwork necessary to relocate them to the United States. Work was an important part of the refugee camp; everyone had to contribute in some way.

Cuong tried to stand, but he was too weak. He thought about Ai' and wondered how she was doing. And then his thoughts drifted to Bian. He wondered again how he was going to tell Ai' about her sister. The thought made him sad and he decided not to worry about it for the time being. He needed to concentrate his energy on getting well and helping Ai'.

The young boy who had helped Cuong off the fishing boat was named Tran Van Danh. He began to feed Cuong some small portions of sea fish. Cuong could not eat as much as he would have liked. His stomach had shriveled from the starvation at sea. It began to hurt after a few pieces of fish. He stopped eating and began asking Danh questions.

Danh was a year younger than Cuong. He had come from a village called Ap Nam in South Vietnam. He also had traveled alone. Danh's family had been killed by the communists. One day the soldiers had stormed his village. Apparently, some of the villagers had fought against the communists and when the communist soldiers found out, they decided to kill them. Danh's father had never fought against the communists, but they killed him anyway because they thought he had. When his mother tried to help his father, the communists killed her also. Danh escaped by hiding in the jungle for two days. It was then that he'd decided to leave his homeland and go to America.

Danh had been living on the island with a family of four. They, like the others, had escaped to Pulau Bidong. Nguyen Huu An, the father of the family, had enough money to purchase his boat as a home. They had lived there for eight months, but Danh told Cuong that some families had lived as refugees as long as a year. Cuong hoped that he would not have to stay on the island that long.

Danh explained that the organization sponsoring the refugee camp, the UNHCR, needed time to locate people in the United States who would help the refugees begin their new lives in a new country. And, because there were so many refugees on Pulau Bidong, it was difficult to relocate everyone immediately.

Cuong asked how Ai' was. Danh told him that there was an American doctor in the camp. They had a small makeshift hospital located in an old warehouse on the island. He told Cuong that Ai' had been taken there and the doctor would take good care of her.

Cuong slept most of that day. When he woke, An, the owner of the boat-home, was back from a day of work in the fields. They talked about their voyages and about their homeland. They each had ideas about what they wanted to achieve in America. Cuong felt comfortable with An; it was the most comfortable he had felt in months. Shortly after Cuong and An had begun talking, An's wife Phuong came home. Phuong worked at the small hospital as a nurse's aid.

She told Cuong that Ai' was doing well, and in a few days she would be able to join Cuong in their home.

Cuong was glad to hear the news about Ai'. He thanked God and promised him that he would take care of her while they were on Pulau Bidong. The thought saddened him. He knew that once he and Ai' were off the island, he probably would never see her again. He wondered about the strange sensation he had felt for Ai'. He first noticed the feeling a few weeks before. He never experienced such a feeling as this. When he was on the boat fighting death from starvation and trying to keep Ai' alive, he'd thought the feeling might have been just compassion for the sick girl. When his feelings about Ai' came to him, Cuong pushed them aside. I will try to understand them later, he thought.

However, Cuong's feelings for Ai' grew stronger. He wondered if what he was experiencing was love. He only knew about love from his relationship with his family. And those feelings were different from what he was feeling for Ai'. He'd never loved any of the girls in his village. He'd liked a few of them. He'd enjoyed running across the rice paddies with them, or catching small fish with their bare hands in the stream that ran behind their village. Cuong realized that whatever it was he was feeling for Ai', he wanted to feel it as much as possible.

A few days later, the immigration officials from the UNHCR came to visit with Cuong. They explained to him how they would try to find a sponsor family for him in America. The officials told Cuong, that there was no way they could determine how long he would have to remain on Pulau Bidong. They told him that they would try their best to relocate him as quickly as possible. There were many jobs available working in the fields and that was where they needed him the most. However, a job would come only when his health had returned.

Cuong had not forgotten his promise to Bian. He wanted to talk to the officials about Hung and his crew, and the way the passengers had been treated aboard the small fishing boat. He wanted them to know about the rape of Bian, and her death. As he remembered the brutality, he became angry. But Cuong knew that it was not a good time to discuss Hung. He was more concerned about his health and the health of Ai'. Hung and his actions would have to wait.

The officials from UNHCR spoke to Cuong about the hazards of the island. He listened intently as they discussed the black market that thrived there. It appeared that any article that was of value was a market for smugglers. Cuong was told how local fisherman would anchor their small fishing boats just off the island full of articles like cigarettes, lighters, clothing, and even drugs. Young Vietnamese refugees would then swim out to the boats, carrying enclosed, airtight containers. Once aboard the fishing boats, the fisherman would sell the goods to the young boys. The youths would swim back to the island carrying their contraband to be sold on the island on the black market.

It was a dangerous swim to and from the boats. Many of the boys drowned. The tides off the island of Pulau Bidong were swift and unpredictable. Even the strongest and bravest of the young swimmers struggled to make the round-trip swim, especially when carrying a container of black market goods. The immigration officials warned Cuong not to involve himself with any of the smugglers. If he did, it would mean a jail term and a trip back to Vietnam. They also warned Cuong about the gangsters, black market vendors, and prostitutes that lived on the island. They told him that at some time, he would probably be approached by one of them, and, it would be best to ignore them.

A week after Cuong and his fellow passengers had arrived at Pulau Bidong, Ai' was released from the hospital. Cuong had already begun to visit her. He was amazed at how fast she had regained her strength. She was even prettier than when he had first seen her, sitting next to Bian, on the tiny fishing boat. He noticed how Ai's skin had returned to its smooth, white texture. Her appetite had returned and she had gained back some of the weight that she'd lost. Cuong was happy to be with her again.

Ai' had been asking Cuong how Bian was, and why she had not seen her. But he had not yet told her the truth about Bian. Afraid for her health, he wanted to wait until she was strong enough for the news. He had been telling Ai' that Bian was happy, and she had been well taken care of. He did not believe that he was lying to Ai'. Cuong believed that Bian was in God's hands.

Thirty-Three

I received a phone call from a man who owned a publishing company in Syracuse. He had read some of the articles that I had written for various treasure-hunting and metal-detector magazines. He told me that he had an idea for a book about the North Side of Syracuse and wanted to know if I would be interested in writing it. I was both shocked and honored that he would ask me to author such a book. I was not a novelist. I thought of myself as a kind of hack freelancer who enjoyed submitting short stories about my metal detecting and treasure-hunting adventures. When I asked my wife what I should do, she told me "to at least listen to what the man has to say." Smart woman!

I met Jerry Damon, a part owner of Parnassus Press, at a North Side eatery called "The Sandwich Shop." After introducing ourselves, we talked for a few minutes about our families and our jobs. Jerry told me that he had moved to the North Side a few years before, but was originally from Long Island where he'd started his publishing company. He had heard of the new developments that had been started in Syracuse. After he researched the area and the history of the city, he thought that perhaps there would be a need for his business.

Jerry began to tell me his ideas about the book. He said he wanted to bring together a story about the North Side's transition from a neighborhood of German, Italian and Polish families to what it is today, a neighborhood for mostly Asian families. He explained that the idea he had for the book's story needed to be told by a person who'd known the North Side of the '50s and '60s. Although excited about the prospect of being the author of such a book, I did have my doubts about the project. Writing a book takes time. And time was not a commodity I enjoyed. I had a financial planning business that kept me busy and was involved with buying and selling first edition books through my website. I was also writing treasure-hunting stories for magazines. So, I was not sure that I had the time to commit to such an undertaking. As I sat there listening to Jerry's ideas for the book, I was not totally convinced. I told him that I needed time to think about his offer and would be in touch with him in a few weeks.

The idea of writing a book about the North Side stayed with me. I was not convinced that I could pull off such an endeavor, but still, I kept thinking about it. I knew that if I committed myself to such a project, I would complete it. Writing a book has always been a dream of mine. I had always admired people who could write books. Sure, I had written a few stories that were good enough to be published in a few magazines. However, a person needs to be a very patient writer if they want to tackle a book project, and I am not a patient individual. The writer of a book needs to be able to stay focused for a very long time, sometimes years. I had trouble staying focused with a thousand-word article for a magazine.

However, there was a side of me that wanted to take on the challenge. I still loved the North Side. I knew that if I could find a way to commit myself to the book, then perhaps I could do it. And then one day something happened that forced me to look at the book project with more of a commitment.

I was driving along a street on the North Side, on my way to meet with Jerry. I still had not made up my mind as to whether I wanted to write the North Side story. I stopped at a convenience store gas station to purchase gas and the daily newspaper. An Asian woman was behind the counter and was waiting on a young boy in front of me. Suddenly, a young girl came running into the store screaming for help. Her face was bloody and badly beaten. She was yelling that she had been attacked by a young man who seemed to be drunk, or on drugs. He'd attacked her as she was walking from her apartment, just a few blocks away, to work.

After the police arrived and had taken a statement from the young girl, they drove her to the hospital. The Asian woman who owned the convenience store told me that she would be selling the business in a few weeks. It had become too difficult for her to continue in the crime-infested neighborhood. She feared for her life and the lives of her husband and two children who also worked at the store.

I left the store and drove to Jerry's office. I told him that I was still undecided as to whether I should commit my time to the book. I said that in all likelihood, I would pass on his offer. I was honest with Jerry, admitting that even though I had to say no, there was a part of me that wanted to tell the story. Jerry was sitting at his desk, his hands folded across his chest. He leaned forward in his chair and rested his arms on top of his desk. He told me there was someone he wanted me to meet and got up from his chair and left the room. In a few minutes, he returned with a well-dressed Asian man. Jerry introduced the man to me as his partner in the publishing company. The man's name was Tran Van Danh.

During the next two hours, I became captivated by the story that Danh told me. He told me about his country of Vietnam and its troubles with communism after the Vietnam War. Danh explained how he'd come to this country and his struggles to survive his journey. He told me about a boat trip on a small fishing boat, and hunger and starvation. He explained about the many deaths he'd witnessed while on the fishing boat. Danh talked about his life at a refugee camp and the struggles he'd had while there. He never smiled while telling his story, not until he began to speak about how his life had changed once he'd arrived in America.

Danh had come to the United States without a family. He had been placed in a sponsor's home for three years. He struggled in school learning the English language. Danh smiled when he told me how he'd worked at two jobs while also attending college. He was proud of the fact that he had received his degree in business in just three years.

Before I knew it, two hours had passed. I was captivated by Danh's story and continued to listen as he related how he had come to live on the North Side. Danh said that after college he'd worked as a manager of a retail store in Syracuse. After a few years, he'd changed jobs to work for the Parnassus Publishing Company where he'd met Jerry. A few years later, Danh bought into Jerry's company and became part owner. Danh was still smiling as he told me how happy he was with his life and how if it hadn't been for the United States, he never would have achieved his dreams.

When Danh had finished telling his story, he looked at Jerry who had been sitting quietly at his desk. The two stared at me, saying nothing. They didn't have to; Danh's story had said it all. I decided to write the book about the North Side, but was not sure where the story would take me. I only knew I had to write it. Jerry, Danh and I talked briefly about how the book would be structured, then we shook hands. I left their office feeling more committed about the book. I drove to the old home where I had grown up. It was just a few blocks from Jerry and Danh's company. I pulled my car into an empty space on Back Alley.

I was parked in front of Axle's house. Turning off the car, I sat staring at Axle's home and then at my old home. Yes, I thought. I will write the book for you my friend. I began to cry. They will not forget you.

Thirty-Four

Danh and Cuong quickly became friends. They worked together in the fields harvesting crops of rice, potatoes, and bean sprouts. In the evenings, both young men and Ai' would walk the beach of Pulau Bidong, or would stroll along the island's streets. Six months had passed since Cuong's boat had arrived on the island. His life, and the lives of Ai and Danh, had slowly bonded into a strong friendship. Cuong and Ai' had also fallen in love.

Cuong had known for a long time that the beautiful girl had captivated his heart. From the first time he had seen her, he'd felt the need to be near her. But it was not until after Cuong had told Ai' of her sister's death that he had realized Ai' felt the same way about him.

On the night Ai' was released from the hospital, Cuong told her how Bian had died. They were sitting in the boat-home with An and Phuong. It was just after dinner, and An and Phuong's two young children had gone outside to play on the beach. Cuong told Ai' everything about Bian's death. Ai' had cried all night. She loved her older sister very much. As children, they had been inseparable—best friends. Ai' could hardly believe the cruelty of Hung and his crew. She'd known that Hung was not a man to be trusted, but for him to have allowed what had happened to Bian was beyond her belief.

In a way, she was grateful that she had been in and out of consciousness. It had saved her from witnessing the horror of her sister's death. But, she also felt guilty for not being able to help Bian. Cuong told Ai' that no one could have helped her sister, and if somehow she'd had the strength to help, she most likely would have met the same fate as Bian. On that day, Ai' became closer to him.

But, the love they shared created a problem. Cuong and Ai' wanted to stay together on the island. They wanted to be together in America as well. The difficulty was that no one knew where they were going to be relocated. Only families could be assured of remaining together. The chances of Cuong and Ai' leaving Pulau Bidong together and going to the same family, or even the same vicinity, in the United States were minimal.

The idea of being separated was depressing for Cuong and Ai'. They had no other choice but to be married. They both agreed that they wanted to spend their lives together. So, because they were both Catholics, the two were married by a Catholic priest just one month after Ai' had been released from the hospital.

Because Cuong had little money to purchase his own shelter for the two of them, they continued living with An and his family. The tiny boat-house was crowded and afforded little privacy for Cuong and Ai'. But that was of little consequence, considering where they had come from and what they had been through.

Cuong and Danh worked every day and were paid weekly in food rations. Luckily, they had few worries while living at the refugee camp. They enjoyed each other's company and would often mingle with the other refugees in the camp. However, some of the others were not to be trusted. Cuong and Danh tried to stay away from them. It was not unusual for them to be approached by individuals who were involved with illegal crimes, such as the black market, drugs, or gambling. All three crimes were punishable by deportation. But even with the strict enforcing of the laws, crime remained a major problem on Pulau Bidong.

Scoundrels had approached Cuong and Danh several times. And, every day there was a murder over drugs, or gambling, or a black market deal that had gone bad. Young Vietnamese children, as well as older men, prowled the streets looking for victims. Cuong had witnessed a stabbing in the field where he worked, and Danh had helped a young boy flee from the hands of a thief in the middle of the afternoon.

In the evening, when the moon was bright, the outline of tiny fishing boats in the water off the beach of Pulau Bidong could be seen. Sometimes, you could see the flailing arms of young swimmers as they made their way to the boats loaded with contraband. Sometimes, the young bodies washed onto the beach. It was on just such a night when Cuong, Ai', and Danh once again came face to face with evil.

They were sitting on the beach. All three were talking about their plans for America. They listened to the waves steadily crash onto the beach. The sky was full of bright stars. Cuong and Ai' were holding hands. Danh was telling them how he wanted to go to the best American college he could. And, how he would work very hard to achieve his dream of some day owning a business in America.

Suddenly, out of the darkness, four men approached the three youths. Two of them were carrying U.S.-issued Army rifles, M16s. The other two men were holding knives with six-inch blades. One of the men, who was carrying a rifle, ordered the three to keep quiet, or they would be killed. Cuong had heard that voice before. He watched the man move toward Ai'. Immediately, Cuong panicked. He recognized the man as Hung. At that same moment, Hung grabbed Ai's arm and began to drag her toward a small outboard-powered boat. The boat was anchored just off the beach.

The two men carrying the knives grabbed Cuong and Danh and began to drag them toward the boat. Ai' tried to scream, but Hung smashed the butt end of the rifle into her stomach. Cuong tried to break free from the grip of the two men, but they held his arms tightly. He could not believe it was happening all over again. He thought that the evil he'd encountered on his journey was behind him. But, as the three of them were dragged toward the small boat, he realized how wrong he had been.

Ai' was still struggling even though pain gripped her stomach as she gasped for each breath. Hung had his right arm wrapped securely around her head. He was covering her mouth with his hand. Hung's left hand had the M16 firmly planted in the small of Ai's back. He continued to drag her closer to the boat. Danh and Cuong were guarded by a young Vietnamese boy who pointed his M16 at their backs as they walked behind Ai' and Hung.

Cuong tried to think of something to do. His mind raced with ideas. He had no idea why they were being taken away. When they reached the small boat, Hung ordered Ai' to quietly climb in. He told her that if she resisted, or screamed, he would cut the throats of her friends. Ai' cried as she looked back at Cuong. Once again Hung smashed the butt of the rifle into her stomach. She toppled forward onto the floor of the boat.

Cuong's rage was immense. He'd hated Hung when he had been a passenger on his tiny fishing boat, but now, his anger was far greater. He'd never realized that he could hate so much. He had hated the soldiers who had taken his brother away to fight, but the anger that he felt toward Hung was much greater. Also, Cuong had never forgotten his promise to Bian and to Ai' that he would some day make Hung pay. Cuong had reported to the officials on the island what had happened to Bian. He'd told them about the hunger and the starvation, and about Hung's total indifference to his passengers. The officials had told Cuong they would investigate the crimes, but they had very little power, or money, to dedicate too much time to probe into all of the allegations of crime the refugees brought to them. Cuong decided that it was up to him to do something about Hung.

As they approached the small boat, Cuong watched the four men closely. He knew that if he was going to act, he needed to do so at just the right moment. He also realized that Hung and two of the others were much older than he and Danh. The youth with the M16 seemed reluctant to be involved with Hung's violence. Cuong knew that if the right moment presented itself, he could overpower the youth. Cuong hoped that Danh would recognize the opportunity to help him.

Danh was also thinking of a way to overpower the men. He had noticed, as well, how timid the young boy was. Danh knew that if he were to try and take a weapon, it would be best to engage the timid youth.

Hung was aboard the boat, pointing his rifle at Ai's head. Cuong and Danh were a few feet away from stepping onto the tiny craft. The young Vietnamese boy with the rifle was standing behind them. One of the older men held a knife to Danh's throat, the other held a knife to Cuong's throat. Hung ordered Cuong and Danh into the boat. He told them to be quiet, or Ai' would die.

In the distance, Cuong could see the outline of a larger vessel. It appeared to be a fishing boat, similar to the type of boat that had brought Ai' and him to Pulau Bidong. Cuong caught Danh's eye and motioned slightly with his head toward the fishing vessel. Danh could see the boat bouncing on the horizon. It was backlighted by the moonlit sky. Cuong and Danh thought the same thing. The boat was probably anchored there waiting for Hung. Danh also knew that his chance must come soon because there might be more men with weapons on the boat waiting in the distance. It would be too difficult to try an escape later.

Cuong and Danh sat next to each other on a wooden seat. They were sitting at the front of the sixteen-foot craft. Ai' lay on the floor at their feet. The young timid boy sat on the seat opposite them, pointing his rifle at their faces. The two older men with knives sat on each side of the young boy, facing Cuong and Danh. Cuong could see that Ai' was in pain. He wondered why she had to go through another ordeal. It made him sick to see her holding her stomach and moaning.

Hung told the youngster with the M16 to point it at Ai' and kill her if Cuong or Danh tried anything. Hung leaned his rifle against his seat. The barrel of the gun pointed toward the sky. Hung turned his back to start the motor. That was the opportunity Cuong had been waiting for.

As soon as Hung turned his back to start the engine, Cuong looked to his right at Danh. Danh knew that Cuong wanted to act. They reacted at the same time. Cuong reached out and grabbed the rifle that was pointed at Ai's head. In one swift motion, he smashed the youngster across the face with the M16 and pointed its barrel at the two older men. At the same instant, Danh jumped over the seat and picked up the rifle that Hung propped up against his seat. Danh pointed the gun at Hung's head and ordered him to turn around and tell his men to drop their knives. Hung made the mistake of laughing. Danh did not hesitate to smash the barrel of the rifle into Hung's stomach. Then, he quickly fired two rounds from the M16 into the air in attempt to alert anyone on the beach. Danh told Hung that if he resisted, or did not turn around and order his men to drop their knives, the next bullet fired would be for him.

In a daze, Hung ordered his men to surrender their knives to Cuong. Cuong, who kept the rifle pointed at the men, told them to throw the knives into the ocean. They hesitated for a moment, and Cuong wasted no time. He pressed the barrel of the rifle against the forehead of one of the men. Once again, he ordered the men to throw their knives overboard. If they didn't, he told them, they would end up as bait for the sharks. The two men gave in to Cuong's request and threw their knives into the ocean. The beach was suddenly filled with people. The police, who had been close by and heard the shots fired from the M16, had arrived first.

Cuong and Danh pointed the M16 rifles at the four men, made them get out of the boat and walked them toward the police. An and Phuong, who also had heard the shots, had run down to the beach, as they knew that Ai', Cuong and Danh had planned to go there. They were shocked when they saw Cuong and Danh marching the four men along the beach. An and Phuong immediately ran to Ai' to help her. Ai' was still in considerable pain from the repeated beating to her stomach. They helped her walk back to the boathouse. She'd survived yet another horror.

Hung and his men were taken to a jail on Pulau Bidong. The police told Cuong and Danh that the men would be taken to the mainland and charged with kidnapping, assault, and other crimes. Cuong also learned that Hung would be charged with piracy and being an accessory to murder in the deaths of Bian and others. The police said they had been watching Hung for months and were building a criminal case against him. He was the ringleader in the black marketing of drugs and prostitution on the island and would be going to jail for a very long time.

The police told Cuong and Danh that Hung probably had wanted to force Ai' to work as one of his prostitutes. Hung usually accomplished this by filling young girls with heroin, making them addicts and dependent on him. As for Cuong's and Danh's abduction, Hung probably would have sold the two boys to the communists, who were looking for escapees to be either executed, as an example for having run from Vietnam, or indoctrinated as communist soldiers. The boys were told that the authorities on the mainland would have a strong case against Hung, and he would be in prison for many years. The police thanked them for their bravery. The two Vietnamese boys earned the respect of the entire island.

Thirty-Five

It took me two years to write the book about the North Side. During that time, I had many meetings with Jerry, Danh and also Cuong about some of the information contained in the story. Cuong's input to the book—details about his life in Vietnam and his escape by boat from Vietnam to Malaysia—was helpful to me as well. Some of the meetings were at Cuong's restaurant, where we would sit and eat, or just sip Chinese tea. I grew to admire the Vietnamese people and their way of life on the North Side. Cuong, Danh and Ai' became my friends.

I never would have imagined that someday I would become friends with people from the country where Axle had been killed. However, I still held my original reasons as to why he had been killed. Axle had died thinking that he was fighting for a just cause, and a worthy goal. Those were beliefs given to him by the politicians and his commanders. However, Axle and every other soldier who died in the Vietnam War died for reasons other than those they were told to be true. Axle died not because the war was about Vietnam, or the United States, or freedom. Axle died because of ignorance. The Vietnam war was ignorant, and that was not Axle's fault. His indoctrination began when the ignorant Army recruiters had told him about the war in Vietnam. The recruiters were not ignorant because they wanted to be; they were ignorant because they had been taught to be that way.

They had been taught how not to think for themselves. They were conditioned to believe everything their country and their commanders told them. It had been pounded into their brains by their drill sergeants and commanders that all young men of fighting age should join the Army and serve Uncle Sam by going to Vietnam to fight and die to stop the spread of communism. Because, if communism was not stopped from spreading in Vietnam, it would slowly creep across the rest of the world, including the United States. That was an ignorant belief. The war was not about stopping communism. The war was about nothing. But, Axle had not known that the war in Vietnam was about nothing when he'd enlisted. He learned about that empty, meaningless war when it was too late for him to change his mind. He heard the term "it don't mean nothin' " many times. It was a term used by the grunts, the GIs, the soldiers, the tunnel rats, and the deserters.

"It don't mean nothin'."

This is what the war in Vietnam was about—nothin', and ignorance. Those were the reasons why Axle and all of the others had died—for nothin'. I wanted to turn those "nothins" into "somethings." I wanted to do something that would mean something to their friends, families, and fellow GIs. They deserved more than a name on a wall, or a small white cross in Arlington National Cemetery. It was the least I could do for Axle and the other heroes who had died because of ignorance.

I decided to dedicate my book to Axle and all of the soldiers who had died in Vietnam. It makes no difference if they were from the North Side in Chicago, the North Side of San Francisco, or the North Side of Syracuse. I wanted all of them to be remembered along with Axle.

Thirty-Six

Their day finally had arrived. Cuong and Ai', along with Danh and two other Vietnamese refugees, were on their way to America. Sponsoring families had finally been located. The five refugees would begin their new lives with different families in New York State. And fortunately, Cuong, Ai,' and Danh would be living in the same city. The city was called Syracuse. The new word sounded strange to the three young refugees. But that didn't bother them. They were glad to be close to each other in the strange new city. Their friendship was just as important to them, as was their new home.

They were flying to the mainland of the Philippines where they would sign more processing papers and then board another plane to America. Cuong, Ai' and Danh had been amazed at their first plane ride. As they'd gazed out of the tiny window and watched the white, cotton-like clouds float by the plane, they talked about how the time they'd spent on Pulau Bidong had prepared them for their life in a new land.

For two years, the three had worked hard at their jobs and learned how to become self-sufficient. They'd learned how to survive in a community of crime and drugs, and how to deal with adversity. They had survived hunger, starvation and even death. Any problems they would face in America would be nothing compared to the problems they had already overcome. They were filled with hope and determination to make a better life in America. Nothing could stop them from achieving their goals.

Cuong talked of saving enough money to bring his mother and father to America, if they were still alive. It had been more than two years since he had left his tiny village and begun his journey to America. He prayed every night that his parents were alive. He wanted them to experience freedom in a new country, as he would.

The friends talked about New York State in America. The UNHCR had mentioned New York as a place in America that featured sponsoring families for Vietnamese. Other than having it shown to them on a map, Cuong, Ai' and Danh had no idea where New York was. But, it did not matter where Syracuse, New York was located, as long as it was a place where one was as free to live as they had been told.

A few weeks before they'd left the refugee camp, and knowing that they soon would be leaving for America, the UNHCR officials had given the three friends books on the English language so they would have a chance to begin to study and understand their new language. During the long plane ride to America, the three friends studied the new and strange sounding English language. They laughed at the different kinds of spelling and the punctuation of each word. They wondered if they were saying the words correctly. No matter how many times they repeated the words using a different punctuation for each one, they never sounded correct.

At times, they would show their books to a flight attendant or a passenger and point to a word on a page. After the correct sounding of the word was given to them, the three would repeat the word to each other. After a while, many of the passengers who were Americans and others who knew the English language would join in and help them. But, Cuong, Ai' and Danh knew that it would take much time and many hours of studying before they would be comfortable with their new language.

Besides the English books, they had been given two hundred American dollars and two sets of new clothes. The UNHCR was poorly funded and was limited as to what they could give each refugee. Besides the clothes, the money and the English book, each refugee had a small personal item or two that they had brought with them from their villages. Each of them had managed to hide these items from the pirates and the thieves who resided on Pulau Bidong. Their personal items from their villages meant a great deal to each of them.

Danh had managed to save a small picture of his family. The picture was torn and faded from the abuse it had received from the salt water and the months of being tucked away in Danh's pocket. Ai' had saved a small lock of hair from each of her family members, except for Bian. Ai' had thought that Bian would always be with her in her new country, so she'd never requested a lock of hair from her older sister. Cuong had managed to hide two items from the pirates. One was a small picture of his parents and his brother. His picture, like Danh's, had been damaged by the long journey. In addition, Cuong had a small pocketknife that his father had given to him just before his journey had started. When the Thai pirates had boarded the tiny boat and began to steal items from the dying passengers, Cuong had managed to hide the knife inside the waste band of his trousers. He had hoped the pirates would not search him as they had the others. Cuong did not want to loose his knife to the thieves.

As Cuong and Ai' stared out the window of the plane, their thoughts were in two separate places. Ai's were of Bian in their village. The two young girls were chasing after a white butterfly as it darted from flower to flower. They were laughing as they tried to catch the elusive insect. They ran from hut to hut, and between villagers, who were almost knocked down by the frolicking girls. Then a tear fell from Ai's eye as she remembered the fun that she and her older sister used to have together. Ai' missed Bian very much.

Cuong was thinking of his village also. He sometimes felt guilty for being the only person in his family to escape his country's terror. Even though his parents had pleaded with him to leave their village and country behind, he could not shake the feeling that he should have stayed behind to help them. He hoped that some day he could forgive himself for leaving his village. Perhaps, he thought, the forgiveness would come when he brought his parents to America.

Thirty-Seven

Just before the book was published, I approached Jerry Damon and Danh and told them that I needed to change the ending. Both were shocked and told me that it was impossible. The publishing date was set and the book was already being edited. In a few weeks the book would be printed. Jerry and Danh also told me that rewriting the ending would be wrong for the story, and they could not imagine any other ending than the one I had already written. I made a case for the rewrite and told them why it was important to the book. To help make it easier for them to agree, I'd brought the new ending with me. They read it, and as I knew they would, both Jerry and Danh agreed with the revision, and the book was published on schedule. Had it not been for a memorable night that I had spent with Cuong and Ai' and their two children at their home, I never would have decided to change the ending.

One evening, Cuong had called me and told me that he wanted to see me. He said that he had something that he wanted to give to me. He asked if my wife and I could come to his home for dinner on the following evening. I accepted his invitation. Cuong was nice enough to make a spaghetti and meatball dinner for me. He even had a bottle of Chianti wine. My wife Debby and I had a wonderful meal and a great time, but things were soon to become even more eventful.

After dinner, we sat in the living room of Cuong and Ai's home. Their two daughters, Hanh, and Da'o, were in their rooms studying, or doing whatever teenagers today do. I was still wondering about what Cuong had wanted to give me. I asked him jokingly if it was the meatballs that he'd given me for supper. He laughed and turned to look at Ai' who was sitting next to him on the sofa. Ai' smiled back at Cuong and nodded her head. My wife and I were sitting on a loveseat opposite Cuong and Ai'. When Ai' nodded at Cuong, he got up from the sofa.

"There are two reasons why you and Deb are here this evening," he said.

Two reasons, I thought to myself. I looked at Deb confused and shook my head. Cuong walked to a large oak hutch and opened the door. I could not see what he had removed from the cabinet. Whatever it was, he put it into his pocket. Cuong continued to stand.

"First, I want to congratulate you on finishing your book." He held up a glass of wine. "To its success," he toasted.

I was embarrassed. I never blush, but I think at that moment I turned as red as the wine I held in my glass. Deb squeezed my hand and kissed my cheek. I thanked Cuong and sipped my Chianti.

"Please. Don't keep stroking my ego," I told him.

Cuong laughed and then sat down next to Ai'.

"I told you that I had something that I wanted to give to you this evening. And, I am about to do that. However, before I do, I would like to explain why I want to give you this item."

I was on the edge of my seat. I told Cuong the suspense was killing me. I told him I loved surprises, just like everyone else. "So, let's not drag this on," I said.

Cuong smiled, sipped his wine, and leaned over to kiss Ai'. Ai' told Cuong to "please hurry up."

"When you gave me the draft of the book to read for my advice I was honored. And then I became surprised." He looked at Ai'. She whispered to him to continue.

"When I read your book, I could not sleep for a week."

"My God, Cuong, is the book that bad?"

Cuong laughed. "Of course not, the book is wonderful."

"I could not sleep because . . ." Cuong stopped talking in mid sentence. Ai' whispered to him that it was okay. She held Cuong's hand as he reached into his pocket. Whatever he held in his hand, I could not see it. He held the item closed in his hand.

"My father gave this to me when I left my village in Vietnam." Cuong had tears in his eyes. I had never seen him so emotional before. And then Ai' began to cry.

I still could not see what Cuong was holding in his clenched fist. But, I knew that whatever it was, it meant a lot to him. Cuong wiped the tears from his face and continued.

"My father fought in the war against the Northern soldiers in my country. He fought along side the American GIs. He told me that he had become friends with many of them." Cuong stopped talking briefly and sipped his wine.

"There was one American GI who he had been particularly fond of."

Cuong stopped talking again. He needed to collect himself. Ai' continued to squeeze his hand and asked him if he was all right.

Deb and I were saddened by Cuong's emotions. But, we were still confused, not sure where Cuong was going with his story, and what it had to do with me. Cuong apologized and once again continued with his story.

"The American GI, who my father was so fond of, was killed in a battle. He died trying to save his sergeant. My father was with him at the time." Cuong held out his hand and opened his fist to show me what he was holding. "This belonged to the GI who was killed. And now, it needs to be with you."

I could not believe what I saw. I know I tried to talk, but no words could be formed. My heart raced as I stared at the red Swiss Army knife that Axle and I had exchanged so many years ago. For a moment, I wondered if I were dreaming.

I stared at the knife in the palm of Cuong's hand. I stared at it for a very long time. And then, Cuong broke the silence and told me to take the knife. As I did, a tear fell from my eye.

The knife was scratched, but still in excellent condition. The inscription was still legible:

"For my friend Dickey Axle Palumbo."

I wiped away a tear that had fallen onto the pocketknife. I was still unable to find words that could sound meaningful. Cuong once again broke the silence.

"My father told me that the young GI who owned the knife had once told him that his best friend had given the knife to him. And that he'd promised his friend that he would never use it, and he would cherish it as a token of their friendship."

I cried as I held the pocketknife in my hand. I thought back to the day when Axle and I had sworn our allegiance to each other by becoming blood brothers. I remembered how we'd cut our fingers and joined them together, in a symbol of our bonding friendship. Cuong spoke again.

"You can imagine how I felt when I read in your book the name of your friend.

"I remembered that name from the inscription on the pocketknife that my father had given to me. At first, I thought it was just a coincidence. But, when I got to the part about you and Axle exchanging the pocket knives, I knew that I had your friend's knife." Cuong looked at Ai' and smiled.

"I knew at once that the Axle in your book was the same person who'd died fighting in my country. He was the GI my father was talking about."

I still could not believe what I was hearing from Cuong. How can this be happening? I thought. Situations like this only happen in the movies, or in books. That was the moment I decided to change the ending to my book about the North Side.

"I never had any doubt whether I was going to return the pocketknife to you," Cuong said. "I just needed the right time to do so."

I smiled at Cuong and told him something that I did not want to say. But I had to. I told him that I could not accept the pocketknife, because it was a gift from his father to him, and I wanted it to remain that way.

Cuong refused and would not take the knife back. I told him that Axle would have wanted him to have the knife. Cuong resisted again.

And so, the small red Swiss Army knife rests on top of my dresser next to the knife Axle had given to me so long ago. They sit side by side as tokens of friendship from a North Side friend.

I can look back now and understand why it was so important for me to walk back through my old neighborhood. And why it was important to visit the home where I had grown up. The layers of guilt are now gone. They were tossed aside years ago.

I never lost Axle as a friend. He remains with me to this day. Nor do I hold any more ill feelings toward the country where Axle was killed. I am older now. And, I understand that sometimes to move forward in life, we have to take a step back, into the past.

The End